It's a battle of the books—
and Amy Anne is determined to win!

It all started the day Amy Anne Ollinger tried to check out her favorite book in the whole world, *From the Mixed-up Files of Mrs. Basil E. Frankweiler,* from the school library. That's when Mrs. Jones, the librarian, told her the bad news: her favorite book was banned! All because a classmate's mom thought the book wasn't appropriate for kids to read.

Amy Anne decides to fight back. Soon, she and her friends find themselves on the front line of an unexpected battle over book banning, censorship, and who has the right to decide what they can read.

"A book lover's book that speaks volumes about kids' power to effect change at a grassroots level."
—*Publishers Weekly*

"A stout defense of the right to read."
—*Kirkus Reviews*

"An inspiring story about 'good trouble' that's worth the consequences."
—*Booklist*

Also by Alan Gratz

The League of Seven
The Dragon Lantern
The Monster War

Ban
This
Book

Alan Gratz

A Tom Doherty Associates Book | New York

This is a work of fiction. All of the characters, organizations, and events portrayed in this novel are either products of the author's imagination or are used fictitiously.

BAN THIS BOOK

Copyright © 2017 by Alan Gratz

Reader's guide copyright © 2017 by Tor Books

All rights reserved.

A Starscape Book
Published by Tom Doherty Associates
175 Fifth Avenue
New York, NY 10010

www.tor-forge.com

The Library of Congress has cataloged the hardcover edition as follows:

Gratz, Alan, 1972– author.
    Ban this book : a novel / Alan Gratz.—First edition.
        p. cm.
    "A Tom Doherty Associates book."
    ISBN 978-0-7653-8556-7 (hardcover)
    ISBN 978-1-4668-8557-4 (ebook)
1. Prohibited books—Juvenile fiction. 2. Censorship—Juvenile fiction. 3. Libraries—Juvenile fiction. 4. Books and reading—Juvenile fiction. 5. Problem solving—Juvenile fiction. 6. Challenged books. 7. Libraries—Censorship. I. Title.
    [Fic]—dc23   2017288884

ISBN 978-0-7653-8558-1 (trade paperback)

Our books may be purchased in bulk for promotional, educational, or business use. Please contact your local bookseller or the Macmillan Corporate and Premium Sales Department at 1-800-221-7945, extension 5442, or by email at MacmillanSpecialMarkets@macmillan.com.

First Edition: August 2017
First Trade Paperback Edition: May 2018

Printed in the United States of America

0   9   8   7

To librarians everywhere

Ban This Book

The Mystery of
the Missing Book

It all started the day my favorite book went missing from the library.

I didn't know it was missing. Not yet. In my mind, it was still sitting there all alone on the shelf like a kid in the cafeteria waiting for her one and only friend to come and find her. Waiting for *me* to find her. All I wanted to do was run to the library and check out my favorite book before homeroom, but Rebecca, my one and only real-life friend, was still talking about trademarking our names.

"Have you ever thought about registering AmyAnne Ollinger.com?" Rebecca asked me.

"No, Rebecca, I have never thought about registering AmyAnneOllinger.com. I am nine years old. Why in the world would I bother to register a Web site with my name on it when my parents won't even let me use Facebook yet?"

That's what I thought about saying. What I said instead was, "No."

"You should," Rebecca told me. "You've got a unique name, but even so, somebody could register it, and then what would you do? RebeccaZimmerman.com is already gone! I'm ten years old, and already my future intellectual property is being snapped up! Jay Z and Beyoncé trademarked their baby's name less than a month after she was born. You'd think my parents would have known enough to do the same."

Rebecca's parents were both lawyers, and she wanted to be one too when she grew up. I couldn't imagine a more boring job.

Instead I said, "Yeah."

I was still itching to get to the library and check out my favorite book. I opened my locker to stuff my backpack inside and gave my mailbox a quick look. Nobody knows how it got started, but everybody at Shelbourne Elementary has these cardboard boxes taped to the inside door of their lockers, just below the little vents they put on there in case you get stuffed in your locker by a bully. If you want to leave a note for somebody you just slip the piece of paper in the slot and it falls right into the little cardboard box. It's such a tradition that Mr. Crutchfield, the custodian, just leaves the boxes in the lockers from year to year.

As usual, my mailbox was empty. Which I'd expected. My one and only friend doesn't believe in writing notes. "Never leave a paper trail," Rebecca says. More advice from her lawyer parents.

"Did you hear about Morgan Freeman, the actor?" Rebecca asked. "Somebody who wasn't named Morgan Freeman registered his name at morganfreeman.com, and he had to sue them to get it back! Now *that's* an interesting case—"

"I can't imagine anything *less* interesting, Rebecca! I don't care anything about trademarks or registering domain names. I have to go check out my favorite book before somebody else does!"

That's what I wanted to tell her. Instead I held up a handful of books like a shield and said, "I have to return these books to the library before class!" and backed away before she could tell me more about the court case. "I'll see you in homeroom!" I called.

Normally I would already have my favorite book checked out and in my backpack, but our librarian, Mrs. Jones, has a rule that you can only renew a book two times in a row, and then it has to sit on the shelf for *five whole school days* before you can check it out again. She says it's to make sure other people get a chance to read it, but I think she made that rule up just to make me read other books, which I would have done anyway.

I dumped last night's books in the book return and waved good morning to Mrs. Jones on the way to the fiction shelves.

"Amy Anne," Mrs. Jones called. "Honey, wait—"

"Just let me grab my book," I called back. I turned into

the H–N shelves and hurried to where I knew my favorite book would be waiting for me.

Only it wasn't there.

I looked again. It still wasn't there. I looked behind the books, in case it had gotten pushed back and was hidden behind the others like they sometimes do, but no. It really wasn't there. But my favorite book was *always* on the shelf. Could somebody else really have checked it out?

I was about to go and ask Mrs. Jones when she turned down the row. Mrs. Jones is a big white lady with short brown hair and rhinestone granny glasses that hang around her neck on a chain when she isn't reading. Today she was wearing a red dress with white polka dots. Polka dots are her thing.

"Where's my book?" I asked her.

"That's what I was trying to tell you, honey," Mrs. Jones said. "I knew you'd come in for it first thing."

"It's been five days," I told her. "I marked it down on my calendar. I get to check it out again after five days. You said so. Did somebody—did somebody else check it out?"

"No, Amy Anne. I had to take it off the shelf."

I frowned. Take it off the shelf? What did she mean, take it off the shelf?

"Why?"

Mrs. Jones sighed and wrung her hands. She looked like she was about to tell me my dogs had died. "Because some parents got together and said they didn't think it was appropriate for elementary school, and the school board agreed with them."

"Wasn't appropriate? What does that mean?"

"It means I can't check it out to you, honey, or to anybody else. Not until I talk to the school board and get this nonsense overturned.

"It means, Amy Anne, that your favorite book was banned from the school library."

Did I Just Say That?

I felt like the carpet under my feet was turning into quicksand, and I was sinking fast. I grabbed hold of the bookshelves so I wouldn't fall over. "But—it isn't inappropriate! It's very appropriate! It's a great book! It's my favorite book!"

"I know, honey. I agree. Nobody but your parents has the right to tell you what books you can and can't read. I promise you, I'm going to fight this. But in the meantime I have to abide by what the school board decides, or I could lose my job."

All I could do was nod. I felt like crying, which was stupid. It was like somebody had come into my bedroom and taken my stuff without asking. Which was even more stupid, because it was a library book. Library books belong to everybody.

"You can help get it back, Amy Anne," Mrs. Jones said.

I wiped a tear from my cheek. "How?"

"There's going to be a school board meeting Thursday

night, and I'm going to be there to tell them all how wrong they are. It'd be even better if they heard it from you."

My eyes went wide. "Me?"

"Just to hear why you like that book so much would mean a lot."

I swallowed hard. "Are you crazy, Mrs. Jones? Me, get up in front of a bunch of adults and tell them why that book is my favorite book? Do you have polka dots on the brain? I can't do that!"

That's what I wanted to say.

Instead what I said was, "Okay."

My Favorite Book
(And Why)

The late bus dropped me off in my neighborhood and I stood by the curb, looking down the street at my yellow house. Inside that house right now were Thing 1 and Thing 2, my two annoying little sisters. I closed my eyes and shuddered at the thought of having to spend one more minute with them. You haven't met them yet, but trust me—if there was a prize for Worst Siblings of the Century, Alexis and Angelina would rank right above Fudge Hatcher, Stink Moody, and Edmund Pevensie—and Edmund Pevensie basically sold his brothers and sisters out to the White Witch for a plate of desserts.

Right then and there I thought about running away from home, just like the main characters in my favorite book.

Did I tell you what my favorite book is? The one that got banned from the Shelbourne Elementary Library? The one I said I would go to a school board meeting and talk about? Out loud? In front of other people? It's *From the Mixed-up Files of Mrs. Basil E. Frankweiler* by E. L. Konigsburg. I like a lot of other books too, especially *Island of the Blue Dolphins, Hatchet, My Side of the Mountain, Hattie Big Sky, The Sign of the Beaver,* and *Julie of the Wolves.* Basically any story where the main character gets to live *alone. Indian Captive* is pretty great too, even though Mary Jemison has to live in an Indian village. But I would rather live with Indian kidnappers than live with my two stupid younger sisters.

I turned away from my house and looked down the road that led out of my subdivision toward the four-lane. Papa Taco, our favorite Mexican restaurant, was just fifteen minutes away by car. I could run away to there. How long would it take me to walk it? I shook my head. Even if I made it, what was I going to do?

In *From the Mixed-up Files of Mrs. Basil E. Frankweiler,* Claudia and her little brother Jamie run away to the Metropolitan Museum of Art in New York City and hide out every night in the bathrooms so the security guards don't find them. I could hide out in the Papa Taco bathroom until they locked up for the night, but then I'd just be stuck in a Mexican restaurant all night. Now, if I could somehow get to the library . . .

My dreams of running away died as my mom's car turned into the subdivision and came my way. I waited until she stopped alongside me and rolled down her window.

"Hey, stranger. Thinking about running away?"

"Of course I was thinking about running away. Every day I stand here and think about how I could fill my backpack with a change of clothes and all the money I have—which isn't much, because you don't give me enough allowance—and ride the late bus until it dropped me off somewhere closer to the mall, where I could sleep every night on the beds in the department store."

That's what I wanted to say. But of course I didn't. Instead I said, "No."

Mom was lighter-skinned than me, with frizzy hair and big dimples in her cheeks when she smiled, like she was now. "Hop in," she said. "How was school?" she asked as we cruised the thirty seconds to our driveway.

I wanted to say, "It was awful! My favorite book got banned and Mrs. Jones asked me to come to a school board meeting and talk about it and I said yes and I don't know how I'll ever do it!" But instead I just said, "Fine."

"Don't put your braids in your mouth," Mom told me for the millionth time. My whole head is covered in braids, some of them with little beads at the bottom. I suck on them when I get nervous. Which is a lot.

Mom pulled in beside Dad's truck. I got out and stood by the car, reluctant to go inside.

"Oh, come on," Mom said. "It's not that bad."

"Oh yes it is," I wanted to say. But of course I didn't.

Ponies and Pink Tutus

Our two huge rottweilers, Flotsam and Jetsam, met us at the door to lick my face. They were so tall they came up to my armpits.

"Off. Off," I said, trying to pet them so they knew I had said hello. They barked and wagged their tails, squirming around in front of us so much I couldn't move. I had to follow my mother like she was an icebreaker ship, pushing past the dogs into the kitchen. Dad was there stirring two pots on the stove and baking something in the oven and making a salad. Dad was tall and thin, with skin as dark as mine and muscular arms from laying bricks all day. He had his opera music playing loud again, some Italian lady singing like somebody was shaking her by the shoulders the whole time.

"Spaghetti in fifteen minutes," he told us. "Alexis!" he yelled. "Come set the table! I've asked her three times."

"I can't!" Alexis called from our room down the hall. "I'm changing for ballet!"

"Amy Anne, will you do it, honey?" Dad asked.

"No. Alexis always has some excuse not to do what she's told. Make her do it." That's what I wanted to say. But I knew from experience it didn't make any sense to argue. It never had. It was easier for everybody concerned if I just went ahead and did it. I dumped my backpack on the floor and went to the cabinet for the plates. Mom disappeared down the hall to change out of her work clothes.

"How was chess club?" Dad asked me, and I cringed a little. I took the late bus home every day because I told my parents I was staying late for different clubs, but I wasn't really in the chess club, or the anime club, or the robotics club. I wasn't in *any* club. I just sat in my favorite corner of the library and read books until I had to leave. It was the only time I ever got any peace and quiet.

"Fine," I lied.

Angelina, my youngest sister, came galloping into the kitchen on all fours. She was a pudgy five-year-old with Mom's dimples, Dad's darker skin, and her hair pulled back into a fuzzy ponytail on the back of her head. Angelina had decided she was going to grow up to be a pony, and for the past few weeks she'd been practicing all day. She made a *pbpbpbpb* sound with her lips and nudged me with her head.

"Hello, Angelina," I said.

"Rainbow Sparkle!" she told me. Rainbow Sparkle was her pony name. I was definitely not calling her Rainbow Sparkle.

The dogs thought Angelina was playing with them, and they started hopping around and barking at her right where I was walking. I had to hold the plates up high not to drop them as I squeezed back and forth. Angelina and the dogs got under Dad's feet, and he stepped back from the stove with a scowl.

"Okay, I need all ponies and dogs out of the kitchen while I finish dinner," Dad said. "Amy Anne, can you do something with them?"

"Why am *I* supposed to do something with them? I'm not the one crawling around on the floor getting them all riled up!" That's what I wanted to say, but of course I didn't. I just grabbed *Roller Girl* out of my backpack, led Angelina into the hall by her imaginary lead, and called Flotsam and Jetsam to follow me to the room I shared with Alexis.

Alexis's clothes were all over the floor of the bedroom— even on *my* side of the room—and she was holding onto the corner of my bed to practice arabesques in her pink tutu. Alexis, the middle sister, was a pretty brown color somewhere between Mom and Dad, and had her pink-highlighted hair cut short and straightened. A pop song blasted from her CD player.

I kicked her clothes across the imaginary line that separated the two sides of our room. "Use your own bed!" I told her for the thousandth time.

"I can't!" she told me for the thousandth time. "Your bedpost is exactly the same height as the ballet barre!"

"Too bad," I said, but she didn't let go. I punched the eject button on her CD player, nabbed the CD, and jumped up on my bed.

Alexis scrambled after me, reaching for the CD. "Mom! Mom, Amy Anne took my music again!" Alexis yelled.

"It's my room too, and I want to read!" I told her.

"Amy Anne," Mom called. *"Amy Anne!* Give your sister back her CD."

"Why? It's half my room too," I wanted to say, "and I don't want to listen to Taylor Swift while I read!" But I knew it wouldn't do any good. Alexis always got to practice her ballet whenever she wanted to. I tossed the CD like a Frisbee onto Alexis's bed, and she dove across the room for it. I called the dogs, and they followed me as I stomped into the hall. Mom had changed clothes and was headed to the kitchen when her phone rang.

"Don't answer that!" Dad yelled.

Mom took her phone out of her pocket and looked at it. "It's the office."

"Definitely don't answer that!" Dad yelled.

Mom answered it. "Hello? Yes? You're kidding. Redo the presentation? Really? *Before the end of the day tomorrow?*

But it's not due until—no—I'm home already. About to sit down with my family and—" She covered the phone with her hand and called out to my dad. "Jamal, can you *please* turn that music down?"

"Told you not to answer it!" Dad said. He didn't turn down the crazy opera singer.

Flotsam and Jetsam tried to run into the kitchen again to mooch for food, and I had to drag them with me into the living room. But I couldn't even hide out there. Angelina had pulled all the cushions off the furniture to make a barn for herself, and she'd used Mom's paper shredder again to slice up paper to make fake hay. Today she'd found something to build a fence out of too.

"My books!" I said. The few books I owned were all propped up against each other in a half circle outside her "barn," the spines twisting out of shape. I started to snatch them up, and Angelina wailed.

"No! *No!* I need those! I need those!" She tried to grab them back from me. "You're not using them!"

"Well, you're not using your room," I told her. "How about I just go in there and read?"

Alexis and I shared a room because five years ago Mom and Dad decided our house wasn't crazy enough and they needed another kid. So Angelina got a room all to herself because she was the baby and had a different bedtime. I would have been happy to go to bed at eight o'clock every night and read if it meant I could have my own room, but I knew there was no way Alexis and Angelina would share a room together.

I marched toward Angelina's room with my armful of books.

"No! No! That's my room! You can't!" Angelina screamed.

Mom stuck her head in the room. "Girls, *please*. I'm on the phone with work."

Angelina wrapped herself around my leg. "Amy Anne took my fence, and now she's going in my room!" she wailed.

"Amy Anne, I need you to be the mature one here," Mom said.

"But—"

Mom mean-frowned at me. "Fix this," she said, and went back to her phone call.

So I had to give Alexis's CD back, but Angelina didn't have to give me my books back? How fair was that? And Mom didn't understand why I wanted to run away.

I turned away from Angelina's room and shoved the books back at her. "Here. And if you bend any of the pages or covers, you're a dead horsey. Understand?"

"*Pony,*" Angelina said, arranging the books back into a fence.

"Amy Anne?" Dad called. "I thought I asked you to keep these dogs out of the kitchen! They're licking the floor again!"

I drooped. The dogs had slipped away from me while I was arguing with Angelina.

"Flotsam! Jetsam! Come!" I yelled.

In the hall, Mom put a finger to her other ear and frowned. "I'm sorry, can you say that again?"

I led the dogs into the bathroom and shut the door. It was the only place left where I could get away from everyone. I sat down on the closed toilet seat with a huff and pulled Jet and Flot to me, hugging them. They were the only ones who ever really listened to me. With everybody else, I'd just stopped trying.

"I don't suppose you guys have found a magical rabbit hole I can fall down or dug up an enchanted amulet in the backyard that leads to another world, have you?"

Flotsam and Jetsam licked my face and wagged their stubby tails, which I took as a no.

"At least we can hide out in here until dinner," I told them.

The door rattled. "Mom! *Mom!*" Alexis yelled. "Amy Anne is hogging the bathroom and I have to pee!"

It Speaks

At dinner, Alexis twirled her spaghetti on her fork like a ballerina, making it plié into the sauce. Angelina whinnied and ate without using her hands. I decided to get on the computer after dinner and look up how far I'd have to walk to run away to the public library.

"This presentation thing means I'm going to have to work late all this week," Mom said. "I'll need you to pick up Angie from Mrs. Taggert's," she told Dad.

"I can do every day but Thursday," he said. "I've got that appointment to see about rebricking that house in North Raleigh. I should be able to take Alexis to ballet though."

Mom sighed. "I'll just have to find someone to cover for me. Anything else?"

"I want to go to the school board meeting on Thursday," I wanted to say.

And this time, I actually said it.

Mom and Dad looked at me in surprise.

"A school board meeting?" Dad said. "Are you thinking about running for office, kiddo?"

"No," I said. "I just need to go."

"Thursday is already very busy, sweetheart," Mom said. "Your dad has his appointment, Alexis has ballet at seven, Angelina has her playdate that afternoon, I've got a big presentation at work due next week—"

"But they're going to ban my favorite book!" I told them.

"Who is?" Dad asked.

"The school board!"

"Why?" Mom said. "Is this something you shouldn't be reading in the first place?"

"No! It's *From the Mixed-up Files of Mrs. Basil E. Frankweiler*. I've read it like a hundred times! But now it's not on the shelf anymore, and it's my favorite book!"

"It sounds like you're pretty fired up about this," Mom said.

I guess I was. Everybody at the table was looking at me. Angelina had even stopped pretending to be a pony.

Mom and Dad glanced across the table at each other, saying something to each other without saying anything like they sometimes do, and Dad said, "I guess I could take her, if you can pick up Angelina and take Alexis to ballet too."

"I can't do both," Mom said. "But we can ask Mrs. Mitchell if Angelina can stay for dinner again. And maybe

Alexis can come back to the office with me until it's time for ballet."

Alexis and Angelina protested—Angelina said Mrs. Mitchell's food was too spicy and Alexis always thought Mom's office was too cold—but Mom and Dad told them they would both survive, and that was that. I was going to the school board meeting.

I couldn't believe it. For once I had actually said what I was thinking and something was happening about it. I felt a little flutter in my chest, like that split second when you're peering over the top of the hill on a roller coaster and then the weight of it grabs you and drags you down, and you're scared but really excited. I wanted to close my eyes and throw my hands in the air and scream, but that might have freaked everybody out.

Then again, maybe nobody here in Crazytown would even notice.

Common Sense

Thursday came quick, and suddenly Dad was driving me to the school board meeting in his truck. The school board meeting where I was supposed to tell everybody why I like *From the Mixed-up Files of Mrs. Basil E. Frankweiler*. With every mile that passed, I regretted opening my mouth a little bit more.

The school board meeting was in a room on the third floor of a big gray building downtown. There was a curved table at the front where some of the school board members were already sitting, and two sections of uncomfortable seats facing them with an aisle running down the middle.

And right at the front of the aisle was a podium with a microphone on it. The microphone I was supposed to get up and talk into.

The folded piece of paper with the speech I'd written about *From the Mixed-up Files* crinkled in my pocket. I've only ever stolen one thing in my entire life—a lollipop from the grocery store when I was four. I'd snatched it while we were in the checkout line and stuck it in my pocket. But I was old enough to know it was wrong, and that lollipop felt radioactive the whole way out the door and into the parking lot. I felt like everybody could see it, like everybody knew I was a bad girl. It burned so hot that I broke down in tears and confessed before we ever got to the car. That piece of notebook paper in my pocket felt like that now. I was surprised it hadn't set off all kinds of alarms on the way into the building. How was I ever going to stand up and read what I'd written in front of all those people?

Mrs. Jones, the librarian, saw us come in and hurried over to give me a hug. She was wearing a black dress with white polka dots tonight, and big black polka dots for earrings.

"Oh, honey, I'm so glad you came tonight," she said. "Amy Anne's our own honorary librarian," she told Dad. "I think she spends more time in the library than I do."

I was suddenly worried Mrs. Jones was going to let it slip that I hung out there every afternoon instead of going to clubs. She didn't know I'd been lying to Mom and Dad.

She held out her hand to Dad instead. "Opal Jones," she said.

"Opal's a pretty name," Dad said, shaking her hand.

Mrs. Jones blushed. Grown-up ladies always act weird

around my dad. Mom says it's because he has bricklayer arms and a movie star smile.

"My parents gave me an interesting first name because our last name was Smith," Mrs. Jones said. "Then I went and married a man named Jones." She shrugged. "What can you do?"

"So what's all this about book banning?" Dad asked.

Mrs. Jones took a deep breath. She had big lungs to fill. "It's not the first time we've had a book challenged in the library. But it's the first time the school board has gone over my head to pull a book from the shelves all by themselves. And it's all because of that woman there."

Dad followed her gaze to a petite, pretty white woman with short blond hair. She wore a matching lavender skirt and jacket.

"She doesn't look like a book burner," Dad said.

"That is Mrs. Sarah Spencer, a pillar of our fair community," Mrs. Jones said. "She's a member of the Shelbourne Elementary PTA, the Shelbourne Elementary Playground Redevelopment Committee, the Raleigh Race for the Cure Foundation, the North Carolina Art Museum board, and the North Carolina State Opera Society."

"Oh," my dad said, suddenly interested because of the opera. My stomach seized up and I grabbed his arm. I did *not* want him to start singing at the school board meeting.

"More importantly," said Mrs. Jones, "Mrs. Spencer and her husband are rich, which means the school board listens to her even more than they listen to *me,* the person they hired to do the job."

I didn't know Mrs. Spencer, but I knew the boy in the seat beside her. His name was Trey. He was in Mr. Vaughn's fourth grade homeroom with me, but he and I had a history. He had the same blond hair as his mom, only messier, and wore an untucked blue polo shirt and jeans. He looked up from the notebook he was drawing in, caught me staring at him, and quickly looked away.

One of the school board members called the meeting to order, and we sat down with Mrs. Jones. The seats in the audience weren't even half full.

The board members talked about some boring stuff that only future-lawyer Rebecca would have been interested in, and then it was time for "public comment." That meant people could come up to the podium to speak. I sank down in my chair a little, the paper in my pocket crinkling louder than firecrackers to me.

"Dr. Opal Jones is our first speaker," one of the school board members said.

I sat up. "She's a doctor?" I whispered.

"Not a medical doctor," Dad said. "Library science, probably."

There were *library scientists*? My eyes went wide as I imagined librarians in lab coats looking at books under microscopes, like crime-scene investigators on TV. Wild-haired library scientists cataloguing books with giant machines that crackled with electricity. Mad library scientists swirling new words around in glass beakers. I was so busy imagining what it would be like to be a library scientist that I missed most of Mrs. Jones's speech.

"But worse than ignoring the Request for Reconsideration forms and the whole system this school board put in place to review challenges to books," Mrs. Jones was saying, "is the larger question of intellectual freedom."

Some of the school board members rolled their eyes and shifted in their seats like we all do in Mr. Vaughn's class when he starts telling us how we're all going to need to know how to use fractions one day, so we better pay attention. Mrs. Jones didn't seem to notice.

"It's our job as educators to expose our children to as many different kinds of books and as many different points of view as possible. That means letting them read books that are too easy for them, or too hard for them. That means letting them read books that challenge them, or do nothing but entertain them. And yes, it means letting students read books with things in them we might disagree with and letting them make up their own minds about things, which is downright scary sometimes. But that's what good education is all about."

Some of the school board members were shuffling

papers and checking their phones. None of them seemed to be paying much attention to her.

"Ladies and gentlemen," Mrs. Jones said, "every parent has the right to decide what their child can and can't read. What they cannot do is make that decision for everyone else. I respectfully ask that the school board overturn the arbitrary, closed-door decision to remove these books, and to require any parent still concerned about library materials to follow the established reconsideration policy set up by *this* board. Thank you."

Most of the school board members were looking at the table in front of them when she finished, not at Mrs. Jones. One of them coughed.

"Thank you, Dr. Jones. Mrs. Spencer? You wanted to speak?"

Trey's mom went to the podium. Unlike Mrs. Jones, she didn't have a piece of paper to read from.

"Ladies and gentlemen of the school board, I grew up in this county. I was a student at Shelbourne Elementary once," she said. "And no, I won't say how long ago."

A couple of the school board members laughed.

"Back then, the school library was a safe place. A place where parents could trust that their children weren't going to pick up a book that taught them how to lie, or steal, or cheat. They weren't going to find a book that told them more about their bodies than they were ready to know at the age of ten, or nine, or *five*. They weren't going to find a book that showed them it was all right to talk back and be disrespectful to adults. Call me old-fashioned, but I don't think school should be a place where a parent's authority is undermined. I think it should be a place where it's reinforced."

I frowned. No book I'd read in the library had taught me to lie, to steal, or to cheat! Every kid who had any kind of brains knew how to do all that stuff already. And I was respectful of adults. I always did whatever they told me to do, even when I knew it was a load of pony poop.

"Mrs. Jones never used the word censorship, but it was there behind everything she said," Mrs. Spencer said. "I'm not for censorship. I'm for common sense. We have to protect our children. It's not censorship to keep things away from children that aren't age-appropriate. It's common sense. I'm sure Mrs. Jones wouldn't call it censorship to keep adult magazines filled with S-E-X out of her library."

S-E-X? Who was she spelling that out for? Did she think the kids in the room had never heard the word sex before—or that we couldn't spell?

"This is just eleven books," Mrs. Spencer said. "That leaves thousands more in the elementary school library for our children to enjoy. Far *better* books, too. I have only asked to remove those books that are inappropriate or have no redeeming value. You made the right decision to remove these books from the library, and I hope you can trust in your own wisdom and common sense as parents to see that no child is ever exposed to them again. Thank you."

Beside us, Mrs. Jones cleared her throat and shifted in her seat.

"Thank you, Mrs. Spencer," one of the board members said. "Is there anyone else who wishes to speak to this issue?" he asked.

Mrs. Jones looked over at me and smiled. Dad gave me a questioning look. This was it. This was why I had that piece of paper in my pocket. Why I'd gotten my parents to rearrange their schedules to bring me here. Why I was in a boring meeting room at seven o'clock on a school night instead of sitting in my bed reading a book. They both expected me to get up and say something. To tell the school board why they shouldn't ban *Mrs. Frankweiler*. All I had to do was stand up and walk to the podium.

My heart thumped in my chest and I stared straight ahead.

"Anyone?" the school board member asked again.

The school board waited.

Mrs. Spencer waited.

Mrs. Jones waited.

Dad waited.

I sucked on my braids.

"All right then," the school board member said. "There being no further comment on the matter, I move to uphold this board's decision to remove these books from the Shelbourne Elementary library."

"Seconded," someone said.

No. No! I was supposed to say something. I *wanted* to say something. But I hadn't. I couldn't.

"All in favor?"

"Aye," a bunch of them said.

"All opposed?"

"Nay," two of them said.

"Motion carries. Anyone else have another issue they'd like us to hear?"

And just like that, it was over. One of the other adults in the audience got up to complain about how much homework her kids brought home, but I was barely listening. That was it. My one chance to speak up, my one chance to tell them why my favorite book was so great, and I had done what I always did—I sat there and said nothing. My face was so hot I thought it would catch fire. I grabbed onto the bottom of my metal chair on both sides and hung on. I couldn't even look at Dad or Mrs. Jones.

The school board moved on to talking about bids on plumbers for another school, and my dad huffed.

"I don't think we need to sit around for the rest of this. We've already wasted enough time."

I nodded, trying not to cry.

"I'm going to wait until the end," Mrs. Jones whispered. "Bend the ear of one or two of those board members."

"Good luck," Dad told her.

I looked up at Mrs. Jones as I slid past her down the aisle. "I'm sorry," I told her.

"Oh, there's nothing for you to be sorry about at all, honey," Mrs. Jones said. She took my hand and squeezed it. "You didn't do anything."

"I know. That's the problem," I wanted to say.

But I didn't.

Mixed-up Mrs. Frankfurter

In the car on the way home, I pulled the piece of paper out of my pocket and unfolded it. At the top I had written "Why *From the Mixed-up Files of Mrs. Basil E. Frankweiler* Is My Favorite Book." What I had written below that wasn't long, but it had taken me a long time to do it.

How do you say why you like a thing? You can point to all the good parts. That you like how they ran away from home to a museum. That you like how Claudia packed her clothes in her empty violin case. That they slept in a big antique bed and took baths in the fountain. That they solve a mystery about an old statue. I like all that stuff about *From the Mixed-up Files.*

But none of those is really the reason I've read it thirteen times and still want to read it again. That's something . . . bigger. Deeper. More than all those things added together. How do you explain to someone else why a thing matters to you if it doesn't matter to them? How can you put into words how a book slips inside of you and becomes a part of you so much that your life feels empty without it?

"Is that your speech?" Dad asked. "Why didn't you read it? Dang it, Amy Anne. I thought that was the whole reason we came all the way out here tonight. The whole reason we rearranged everybody's schedules. Your mother and I have a lot better things to do with our time."

Hot tears poured down my cheeks, and I turned away so Dad couldn't see. I tried to swallow a quiet sob, but Dad heard me.

"Are you crying? Oh, Amy Anne, I—dang it. I'm sorry. I didn't mean that. I know how hard it is for you to speak up." He pulled a bright red bandana out of his pocket and handed it to me. "Here, what's the book?"

I shook my head. I couldn't look at him. I was still crying.

"Come on. *Mixed-up Mrs. Frankfurter* or something."

He was trying to get me to laugh, but I was too upset. He was right. Everybody *had* changed their plans for me and we'd come all that way downtown on a school night, and I'd sat there too afraid to say something.

Dad didn't say anything else, but a few minutes later we pulled into the parking lot of the bookstore. I hadn't even noticed we weren't driving home.

"Come on," Dad said. "Clean yourself up now and let's see if they have your book."

Inside, I told the lady at the register the name of the book, and she knew it right away. A few minutes later, Dad bought me my very own copy of *From the Mixed-up Files of Mrs. Basil E. Frankweiler.*

"There you go," Dad said. "Now it doesn't matter whether they have a copy in the library or not. You've got one of your own."

On the way home, I held the book in both hands in my lap. The cover was a little different from the one in the library, and the Newbery Medal on the front wasn't real like the library one. It was just a picture of the medal, not a sticker you could run your fingers over and feel the bumps, even through the clear plastic cover. But that didn't matter, really. The book and the pictures inside were the same.

I was glad to have my own copy, but I couldn't help thinking about that book that wasn't on the library shelves anymore, and how I would never have known *From the Mixed-up Files of Mrs. Basil E. Frankweiler* was my favorite book if I hadn't found it there in the first place.

The Girl with the Mullet

Sometimes I like to pretend I'm the main character in a book. My mom and dad and sisters and Rebecca are all characters too, and Mrs. Jones maybe, and Mr. Vaughn, my teacher, and the other kids in my class. But I'm the main character. I'm the one who explains everything that's happening in my own voice, the one things happen to. The only problem is, the best books aren't the ones where stuff just happens to the main character. The best books are the ones where the main character *does* something, like run away to the Metropolitan Museum of Art. And that's why I could never really be the main character in a book.

I never *do* anything.

I stuck my bookmark in *From the Mixed-up Files* right at the point where Claudia and Jamie collect $2.87 in coins from the restaurant fountain in the museum, and watched out the window of the bus as it took me to school.

I'd already read all the way through my new copy of *From the Mixed-up Files* once already, before I went to bed.

We stopped at Rebecca's house, and she flopped down in the seat next to me.

"How was the school board meeting?" she asked.

I shrugged. "You would have liked it. They said 'make a motion' and 'I second that' a lot."

"*Robert's Rules of Order*," Rebecca said. "That's what they're called. It was written by Robert Somebody-or-other."

"No kidding," I thought, but I didn't say so.

"Did you read the thing you wrote?" Rebecca asked.

I looked out the window. "No."

"Amy Anne! You worked all week on that!"

I shrugged.

"Mrs. Jones talked though, right? What happened?"

"Nothing. All the books are still banned."

Rebecca saw the book in my hand. "Isn't that one of them?"

"Yeah. My dad bought it for me."

Rebecca took the book from me and looked at the cover. "You're all the time talking about what a great book this is. What's so bad about it?"

"Nothing!" I told her. "That lady said it teaches kids to lie and steal and cheat, but they don't do any of that stuff." Only, now that I thought about it, they *do* lie about running away to the museum. And Jamie does cheat at cards. And I guess you could call it stealing when they take the coins from the fountain. "Well, they kind of do, I guess," I said.

Rebecca's eyes lit up. "Cool. Can I read it?"

I was surprised. All the times I'd talked about *From the Mixed-up Files,* Rebecca had never once been interested in reading it. Until now.

"Okay," I said. I pulled my bookmark out and gave it to her. "Only, don't lose it."

Rebecca looked pleased with herself. She started flipping through it to look at the pictures. I grabbed the book and closed it.

"Don't look ahead! You'll spoil it."

Danny Purcell leaned over the back of our seat. "Hey! Are you guys talking about the books Trey's mom got banned?"

Rebecca blushed the way ladies do around my dad. She liked Danny, only she never said so. But sometimes when I was talking to her in class and I realized she wasn't listening, it was always because she was watching Danny. I didn't get it. Danny was nice, and he was good at sports in gym class, but all he really seemed to care about was his hair. He had a big football helmet of hair that he wore down to his eyes like the frosting on a cupcake, and he was all the time combing it down with his fingers to make sure it was swirling the right way.

"I saw the list in the newspaper," Danny said.

"You read the newspaper?" I thought, but I didn't say it.

"I read that list," Danny said, "and I realized, I know one of these books, you know? Like, not from class. It took me a while, but then I remembered why. We own one of them. It's on this bookshelf in my house. It's been there like forever."

I perked up. "Which one?"

Danny threw his head back to flick his hair into place. "Something about waiting for a girl? I don't remember. But the cover has this girl with a mullet talking to a ghost."

"What's a mullet?" I asked.

"It's when your hair's short in the front and the sides but long in the back," Danny explained. The hair expert.

"Girls don't wear mullets," Rebecca said.

"Well, this one does."

I tried to remember the other books on the list. "Is it . . . *Wait Till Helen Comes*?"

"That's it! Mom said it was like her favorite book when she was a kid. Man, I hope she never had a mullet. That is *not* a good look."

Wait Till Helen Comes was one of the books on the list I hadn't read.

"Can I borrow it?" I asked.

Rebecca and Danny both looked at me in surprise.

"Um, sure. Yeah," Danny said. "I'll bring it tomorrow."

Rebecca looked lasers at me, like I was interested in Danny too.

"I just want to read the book," I told her.

"I want to read it too!" she told Danny.

I squinted at her. Did she really want to read it, or was she just saying that because of Danny?

Danny shrugged. "Okay. Sure. I'll bring it tomorrow."

"You can read it after me," I told Rebecca. "You've got *From the Mixed-up Files of Mrs. Basil E. Frankweiler* to read first."

"Why do you guys care so much?" Danny asked. "Are these books really good or something?"

"They have to be," Rebecca told him. "Why else do you think they banned them?"

It took a few seconds, but the truth of that finally got through Danny's thick helmet of hair. He nodded. "Yeah. Yeah, I bet they're *full* of good stuff. Like all those channels my parents block on the TV."

"You can borrow this one when I'm finished with it," Rebecca said, waving *From the Mixed-up Files* under his nose.

Now it was my turn to shoot lasers from my eyes. Who said she could loan my books out to other people?

"All right, cool," Danny said, and he sat back in his seat. I lifted my hands at Rebecca as if to say, "What gives?" but she just blushed again. Whatever. At least now I could be sure she would actually read it.

The bus pulled up to the school and I hauled my backpack into the aisle. That's when I saw who'd been sitting in the seat in front of us. Trey! He must have gotten on while I wasn't watching. How long had he been sitting there? Had he heard us talking about his mom and the banned books? Had he heard me loaning mine out, and asking to borrow Danny's?

Trey flipped a sketchpad closed, put it in his backpack, and slid out past me. He gave me a quick look as he went by, but didn't say a word. What was that supposed to mean? That he *had* heard us? Was he going to rat us out to his mom?

Danny nudged me along, and I followed Trey off the bus. I was being stupid. So what if we were reading the books Trey's mom had banned from the library? They weren't library books. They were *our* books. And nobody but my parents could tell me what books I could and couldn't read. Mrs. Jones had said so.

Which gave me an idea.

The Big Idea

Like the main character in a book, I was finally going to *do* something. I was going to read every book Mrs. Spencer and her friends had banned from the school library.

I found the list in the newspaper in the library, just like Danny said:

Are You There God? It's Me, Margaret by Judy Blume
Scary Stories to Tell in the Dark by Alvin Schwartz
Matilda by Roald Dahl
Harriet the Spy by Louise Fitzhugh
Wait Till Helen Comes by Mary Downing Hahn
It's Perfectly Normal by Robie H. Harris
From the Mixed-up Files of Mrs. Basil E. Frankweiler
        by E. L. Konigsburg
All the Junie B. Jones books by Barbara Park
All the Captain Underpants books by Dav Pilkey

The Egypt Game by Zilpha Keatley Snyder
All the Goosebumps books by R. L. Stine

It wasn't exactly eleven books, like Mrs. Spencer said. It was way more than eleven books when you counted all the gajillion Goosebumps books and the big shelf of Captain Underpants and Junie B. Jones books.

I had already read five of the books on the list, if you count reading a couple of Goosebumps and a couple of Junie B. Jones books. The others I'd read were *Matilda* (awesome), *Harriet the Spy* (awesome), and *From the Mixed-up Files* (super-awesome, of course). I'd never heard of *It's Perfectly Normal* or *The Egypt Game*, but *The Egypt Game* sounded especially good. *Scary Stories to Tell in the Dark* and *Wait Till Helen Comes* I'd seen on the shelf, but I'd never checked them out because they looked scary, and I'm not a big fan of scary books. But I was definitely going to read *Wait Till Helen Comes* now. I hadn't read Captain Underpants either, and I didn't want to. Captain Underpants was stupid. I would read that one last.

The only book I was worried about was *Are You There God? It's Me, Margaret.* I knew that book, of course. It was on the shelf right beside Judy Blume's other books, like *Tales of a Fourth Grade Nothing* (awesome) and *Superfudge* (awesome). Shelbourne Elementary goes up through sixth grade, so some of the books in the library are for older kids. *Are You There God?* had a cover that said sixth grade to me and I'd heard older girls whispering about it in the school bathroom, so I'd always stayed away from it. But I was resolved. I was going to read each and every one of the books Mrs. Spencer said I couldn't, just to spite her. I knew she'd never know, and that it wasn't like I was doing something that would help Mrs. Jones get the books back on the shelves. But I still felt a secret thrill at doing something an adult told me not to do.

That afternoon I emptied my piggy bank out (not breaking it like Jamie did in *From the Mixed-up Files*) and counted it up. Twenty-one dollars and seventy-six cents. That was enough for two paperbacks at least. I asked Mom and Dad if we could go to the bookstore that night, and their reaction was exactly what you'd expect:

"Are you sure that's what you want to spend your money on?" Dad asked.

Why do parents always say that when you tell them you want to buy something with your own money!? I knew what he really meant. He meant, "I don't think that's how you should spend your money."

"Yes. That is what I want to spend my money on," I thought, and this time I actually said it.

Mom and Dad had one of those silent conversations with their eyes again, and Dad sighed and said he'd run me to the bookstore after dinner.

"I need new shoes at the ballet store," Alexis said.

Angelina hopped up and down. "I want to go for frozen yogurt!"

"I need to hit the office store," Mom said. "If we left now, we'd just have time to grab tacos and do all four."

Suddenly my trip to the bookstore had become a family outing. Before I could even think something I wasn't going to say, Dad was fishing his keys out of the bowl by the door and the dogs were barking and whining about us leaving.

Alexis, Angelina, and I climbed into the back of our car. Angelina's car seat was in the middle. I squeezed into one of the other sides, pushing toys and Cheerios onto the floor. The whole car still reeked of spoiled milk from the drink Angelina had spilled a month ago, and before we had even left the neighborhood Thing 1 and Thing 2 were whining.

"The sun is on me!" Alexis said. "I'm hot!"

"You can sit on the other side when we leave the office store," Dad told her. Which meant *I* was going to have to sit on the hot side in the sun, but no one cared about that.

"Amy Anne is touching me!" Angelina whined. "Mom, Amy Anne is touching me!"

"Amy Anne, please don't touch your sister," Mom said.

"Her car seat takes up half the backseat! How am I *not* supposed to touch her?"

"*Amy Anne,*" Mom said.

I crossed my arms and slouched against the car door,

trying to get as far away from Princess Angelina and her throne as possible. Now do you see why I never say anything? Nobody ever listens anyway.

"We're not going to be at the bookstore too long, are we?" Alexis said.

"Not too long, no," Dad said. "Not if we want to get all the other things done and be home before bedtime."

Going to the bookstore was the whole reason we were going out in the first place, and now it was something we had to squeeze in so there'd be time for frozen yogurt! I closed my eyes and breathed deep. It didn't matter. I had enough money in my pocket for two paperbacks at least, and I already knew what books I wanted. Danny was going to loan me *Wait Till Helen Comes,* so I was going to buy *The Egypt Game* and *It's Perfectly Normal,* whatever that was, and I was going to read them both that very night.

NOT A NOVEL

So, it turns out *It's Perfectly Normal* is *not* a novel.

It's a nonfiction book all about S-E-X, as Mrs. Spencer would say.

With pictures.

The Wendigo

I was so embarrassed when I saw what *It's Perfectly Normal* was about. I had even asked somebody at the bookstore to help me find it! I could have died. As soon as I saw what it was, I put it back on the shelf really fast and ran away. I mean, there's stuff in there I do have questions about, and Mom and I have already talked about some of it, but I was *not* going to buy that book with my family right there!

Instead I bought *The Egypt Game* (which *was* a novel) and *Scary Stories* (a bunch of short short stories), and read them both that night.

Wow.

The Egypt Game was great. It's about these kids who build this pretend Egyptian altar in a creepy guy's backyard, and then mysterious things start happening. Like, maybe the Egyptian god is leaving them messages. I guess it got banned because somebody didn't like the kids worshiping Egyptian gods, even if it was pretend. And there's somebody attacking kids in the neighborhood too, which is kind of scary. But the book was really awesome.

Scary Stories to Tell in the Dark I read in the dark, in bed, which was a mistake.

Oh. My. Gosh. I'm still shaking. There's a story in there called "The Red Spot," about a girl who has a spider crawl on her face. That's bad enough (Aaaaaaah!), but the spider bites her or something, and it leaves a big red spot on her cheek. Her mom says it'll go away, but it doesn't—and a few days later it explodes and hundreds of baby spiders come crawling out!!!!! Of her face!!!!!! And even worse, there are these creepy pictures!!! I called the dogs to come and sit with me in bed while I read it, but even that didn't help. In another story called "High Beams," a woman driving a car at night can't figure out why the car behind her keeps flashing its high beams at her. It turns out a killer snuck into the backseat of her car and the other driver saw it, and every time the killer rises up to attack her the car behind her turns on its high beams to stop him!

"Mom! Amy Anne still has her light on and I can't sleep!" Alexis called, making me jump. Mom appeared at our door looking tired. "Amy Anne, you know I don't mind you reading, but Alexis needs her sleep, and you do too."

I nodded and pulled my blankets up high over me. I was shaking so badly I could barely hold my flashlight, but I still wanted to read another story. I turned to one called "The Wendigo." It was about a man and his guide hunting in a part of Canada where nobody else ever goes. One night the wind starts calling the name of his guide, and something comes swooping down out of the dark and snatches him up and flies away with him! The guide screams something about his feet being on fire, and then he's gone. The hunter splits, but later on he's by a campfire when a strange man wrapped up in a blanket sits down next to him. The hunter is sure it's his old guide, the man who disappeared that night. The hunter can't see his face, and the strange man won't answer any of his questions. The hunter decides to lift the man's hat off his head, and underneath he sees—

"Mommmmm! Amy Anne is reading with her flashlight!" Alexis cried, and I screamed and exploded out from under my blanket. Alexis screamed because I'd surprised her, and the dogs went crazy barking like the mailman had suddenly appeared in the room, and the whole ruckus brought Mom running.

"What's going on in here?" she asked.

"Nothing," I whispered, hugging Flot and Jet with both arms. Across the room, Alexis stared at me in horror.

Mom frowned. "Whatever's going on, I need lights out and for you both to go to sleep."

I nodded, and Mom left. I clicked my flashlight off

and stuffed *Scary Stories to Tell in the Dark* under my mattress where I couldn't see it. I finally got Flotsam and Jetsam settled back down and pulled my blanket up over my head, but I knew I wasn't getting to sleep that night.

Or maybe ever again.

Our Own Little Book Club

Danny Purcell brought *Wait Till Helen Comes* on Monday, and I read it that night. It. Was. Awesome. It was scary, but not *Scary Stories to Tell in the Dark* scary. The little girl in it, the one with the funny haircut on the cover, is so creepy! She hates her new stepbrother and stepsister, and she tells them a ghost she met in the graveyard is going to come after them and punish them for being mean to her.

When Rebecca finished *From the Mixed-up Files* (which she liked, mostly I think because Mrs. Frankweiler is all the time talking to her lawyer), she read Danny's copy of *Wait Till Helen Comes* while Danny read *From the Mixed-up Files*. It's like we had our own little book club.

Rebecca caught me at my locker at the end of lunch one day. "Amy Anne! I looked all over for you in the cafeteria. Where were you?"

"I got a pass to go to the library instead," I told her.

Even though my favorite book still wasn't on the shelf, there were lots of other library books I wanted to read.

"Oh, I see how it is," Rebecca said, pretending to be angry. "You love books more than your best friend. Well I don't need *you*. I've got Helen. She's my only *real* friend, even though nobody else can see her. You just wait till Helen comes, then you'll be sorry!"

We cracked up laughing together.

Danny loped over to us and brushed his hair out of his eyes. "Hey! What's so funny?"

We could barely answer him we were laughing so hard.

"Just wait till Helen comes," I said, trying to sound spooky. "Then you'll be sorry!"

"Is that from that book?" Danny said. "No fair joking about it before I've read it! I only just finished *Basil E. Frankweiler*! And I want to read that *Scary Stories* book next."

I froze and shook my head, my eyes wide. "I hid it," I told him.

"Why?" Danny said. "Is it really scary?"

I let out a little squeak.

Danny pulled my locker door open wide. "Where is it? I want to read it!"

The book wasn't in my locker. It wasn't under my mattress anymore either. I hadn't been able to sleep knowing it was there. Right at that moment it was hidden in an old gym bag at the back of my closet, buried under a pile of clothes.

I grabbed my locker door to close it and explain why *Scary Stories* wasn't there, and that's when I saw it.

There was a note in my locker mailbox.

A Notable Note

I didn't notice it right off, because I had gotten used to not getting any notes. But something white and folded was definitely sticking up out of my locker mailbox. I must have stood and stared at it for a long time, because Rebecca had to wave her hand in front of my face to get my attention.

"Hey, earth to Amy Anne! You look like you just saw Helen's ghost."

I pointed to the note. "Did you send me a note?"

Rebecca shook her head. "Never leave a paper trail," she reminded me. Then a horrible thought struck her and she turned on Danny. "You didn't send her a note, did you?"

Danny took a step back. "Hey, whoa. Send a note to a girl? No way."

Rebecca relaxed. If Danny *had* written me a note, I don't know which of us she would have killed first.

"Who else would send me a note?" I asked.

"Well, I know a good way to find out," Danny said. "You could, you know, read it and find out."

I pulled out the note and unfolded it. It was a piece of notebook paper torn out of a spiral notebook, with pink loopy handwriting on it.

> AA—
> Danny said you have The Egypt Game. *Can I read it?*
>
> *—Janna*

"It's from Janna Park," I said. "She wants to borrow *The Egypt Game.*"

"Oh yeah. I told her you had a copy," Danny said.

My heart skipped a beat. Janna Park had written me a note. Janna Park had written me a note and called me AA. No one had ever called me AA before.

I liked it.

Janna was one of the girls who was always following Danny around, like Rebecca. Janna probably liked Danny's hair as much as he did. I was surprised he'd even mentioned *The Egypt Game* to her, since he'd only heard me talking to Rebecca about it on the bus. But I was excited that someone else wanted to read it. Good books shouldn't be hidden away. They should be read by as many people as many times as possible.

I wrote a note back to Janna and stuck it in her locker before going back in to class.

Janna—
Sure. I'll bring it tomorrow.

—AA

Janna came to my locker the next day after lunch. I passed her *The Egypt Game* in secret, like we were in a spy movie.

"Thanks," she said. Then she stood there and didn't leave.

"You're welcome," I said.

She still didn't leave.

"What is it?" I asked her.

Janna looked around, then said quietly, "Do you have any of the other books? You know, if I wanted to read any of them?"

"Oh. Oh, yeah!" I said. "I've got *From the Mixed-up Files of Mrs. Basil E. Frankweiler,* and *Scary Stories to Tell in the Dark,* but it is *really, really* scary. And Danny's got *Wait Till Helen Comes.* But he probably already told you that."

"Oh," Janna said. "Is that all?" She looked in my locker, as though the other books might be in there. She was disappointed, I could tell, and suddenly the only thing

I wanted in the world was to please her. Because she had written me a note and called me AA.

"Those are the only ones I have now," I told her. "But if there's another one you want to read, I can probably get it. I'm saving up." I ran through the titles in my head. "Is it *Are You There God? It's Me, Margaret*?"

She shook her head, and I felt a little relieved. I was still a little afraid of that one.

"Is it . . . *Harriet the Spy*?"

She shook her head.

"Goosebumps?"

No.

"Junie B.?"

No.

"*Matilda*?"

No.

What else could it be? It couldn't be Captain Underpants. That only left . . .

Oh.

Oh.

She wanted to read *that* one.

Rebecca popped up beside us, and Janna and I jumped.

"'Kay thanks bye!" Janna said, and she hurried away.

"What was that all about?" Rebecca asked.

"Janna borrowed *The Egypt Game* from me. But I think she wants to read a different one of the banned books instead."

"Which one?"

I whispered. "The sex book. *It's Perfectly Normal.*" I grabbed a braid and held it close to my mouth. "But I can't buy that one!"

"That was on the list?" Rebecca said. "You don't have to buy that one. I've got it."

My eyes went wide. She had a copy? "At your house?" I asked.

"Yeah," she said. She acted like it was no big thing. "My mom gave it to me. I think that way I couldn't sue her one day for not telling me everything before I needed to know it."

"Have you read it?" I whispered.

Rebecca leaned in breathlessly. "Some parts."

I wanted to ask her which parts, and what it said, but I was too embarrassed. I jumped as Mr. Vaughn called us into class down the hall.

"Will you bring it?" I asked her as we ran to class.

Rebecca stopped at the door. "Okay," she said with a secret smile, and she threw open the door and ran inside.

With Rebecca's book, and Danny's book, and my books, I could have almost half the books Mrs. Spencer banned from the library sitting in my locker by tomorrow, where *anybody* could read them, not just me.

Which is when I got an even bigger idea than the one I had before.

The Bigger Idea

I cleared out the shelf in my locker. On it I put my copies of *From the Mixed-up Files of Mrs. Basil E. Frankweiler* and *Scary Stories to Tell in the Dark* (shiver!), Danny's copy of *Wait Till Helen Comes,* and Rebecca's copy of *It's Perfectly Normal* (which I had only peeked at). Janna let me have a couple of old Junie B. Jones books she had at home, and Danny got his friend Parker to donate his whole collection of Goosebumps books. When Janna gave me back *The Egypt Game,* I would have a total of fourteen books.

Fourteen books banned by Mrs. Spencer and her friends, free to borrow for any student who wanted to read them.

And that's how the Banned Books Locker Library began.

I still had four books to go to have all the banned books—well, more than that, if you counted all the other

Goosebumps and Junie B. books and Captain Underpants books. But all I really still needed was *Harriet the Spy; Matilda; Are You There God? It's Me, Margaret;* and a Captain Underpants book. Then I'd have at least one of everything on Mrs. Spencer's list.

But Mrs. Spencer wasn't done.

When I went to the school library after school to hide out in my usual spot until the late bus came, Mrs. Spencer was there. Today she was wearing one of those pink matching track suits that nobody really goes running in.

And she had another list of books.

"More?" Mrs. Jones said. Her face turned the same color as her orange-and-white polka-dot dress. "Honestly, Mrs. Spencer. Have you read all these books? Have you read *any* of them?"

I pretended to be interested in the magazine rack near the front desk so I could listen.

"I don't need to read them," Mrs. Spencer said. "Once I took my concerns to the school board, a number of other parents brought other books to my attention. I looked up reviews of the books online and decided these books weren't appropriate for an elementary school library."

"*You* decided," Mrs. Jones said. "I didn't realize you had a Library and Information Science degree."

Mrs. Spencer stood straighter. It added an inch to her height, but still not enough to come up to Mrs. Jones's level. "I don't need a fancy library degree to know what's right and what's wrong for children."

"I see," Mrs. Jones said. "Let me just get you some Request for Reconsideration forms then."

"That won't be necessary," Mrs. Spencer said. "I've already spoken to members of the school board about these books, and they agree that they have no place at Shelbourne Elementary."

"Well," Mrs. Jones said, "be that as it may, until I hear from the school board, these books will stay on the shelf." She handed the list back to Mrs. Spencer.

"I see," Mrs. Spencer said. She looked at the list for a moment, then smiled sweetly. "You know, before I go, I think I'll pick out some books to check out. For Trey."

Mrs. Jones smiled back. "Anything I can do to help?"

"No thanks," Mrs. Spencer said. She held up the piece of paper with the new books she wanted to ban written on it. "I have a list."

I knew what Mrs. Spencer was doing. So did Mrs. Jones. Mrs. Spencer was going to check out all the books on her new list so no one else could check them out until the school board told Mrs. Jones to take them off the shelf. And there was nothing Mrs. Jones could do about it. For the next fifteen minutes, Mrs. Spencer went through the shelves and collected every single book on her list. I couldn't watch. But I also couldn't hide out in my favorite spot.

Trey was sitting in it, drawing in his notebook.

I pulled up short, as shocked as I had been when *Mrs. Frankweiler* had gone missing. I felt the heat rise in my face. First Trey's mom had banned my favorite book from the library, and now Trey was sitting in *my* library seat. And I still hadn't forgiven him for what he did to me in third grade. My fists clenched at the hem of my skirt, but I slipped away down a row of books before he could look up and see me.

Mrs. Spencer finally came up to the counter with a huge armful of books, and Mrs. Jones had no choice but to check them out to her in Trey's name.

"Trey, it's time to go," Mrs. Spencer said. He collected his stuff and left my spot at last. On the way out he glanced up and saw me watching him from behind a big potted plant. I stuck my tongue out at him, but he just chuckled.

"That odious woman," Mrs. Jones said when they had gone. "This all started when she didn't like the Captain Underpants book Trey checked out." She gave me an exasperated sigh, but then she seemed to get an idea. She smiled to herself and went into the office in the back, the one with all the windows, and got on the computer.

While Mrs. Jones wasn't looking, I snatched the list

Mrs. Spencer had left on the counter and dashed out of the library. I needed it.

Every time Mrs. Spencer took a book from the school library, I was going to add a book to my secret locker library.

Violent Criminals

Standing next to my locker a few days later was a third grader wearing a tan trench coat with the lapels turned up. He wore sunglasses, and his brown hair looked like a comb hadn't touched the kid's head in days.

"Psst. Psst," he said. "You Amy Anne Ollinger?"

"Yeah. Who are you?"

"Wiebe," he said. "Nikoli Wiebe." He leaned closer. "The red dog barks at midnight," he whispered.

"What?"

He frowned. "It's a code. A spy code."

"Well, it's not a very good code if only one of us knows it," I thought, but I didn't say it.

The boy sighed. "I'm looking for a book. A *secret* book. A *spy* book."

"You mean *Harriet the Spy*?"

"*Shhhh!*" he said. He glanced around like there were spies everywhere.

"It's checked out," I told him.

I opened the B.B.L.L. (the Banned Books Locker Library) to show him. There were only six books left on the shelf. Everything else had been checked out. And even after I'd added another twelve books from Mrs. Spencer's new list. Mostly with Danny's help. He knew all kinds of people who had copies at home.

"I can put you on the list," I told Nikoli. I pulled out the clipboard where people could reserve a book and had him add his name. Whenever somebody turned a book back in, I went through the list and found the next person who wanted it, then left them a note in their locker mailbox saying it was ready for pickup. My own locker mailbox had three notes in it, all from different people in my class, and all asking to read one of the books.

My locker mailbox was getting a lot more use lately.

"You should have a list," Nikoli said. "Of all the books you have. So people know what they can check out."

"And do what? Hang it on the outside of my locker with a sign that says, 'Here are all the books we're not supposed to read that I have hidden in my locker'?" I wanted to say.

Instead I said, "I'll think about it."

Nikoli pulled a pen out of his pocket and talked into it like it was a microphone. "Abort mission. Repeat: abort mission. Alert Ukrainian Intelligence the package is not in the locker. Repeat: not in the locker."

I closed my locker and saw someone watching me from behind another locker door farther down the hall.

It was Trey.

There really were spies everywhere!

"Hey. I got you a new one," Danny said, making me jump. Nikoli was gone, and Danny stood in his place. With one hand he combed his helmet of hair into the exact place he wanted it, and with the other he slid me a beat-up old paperback copy of *My Brother Sam Is Dead*.

I squeaked and stuck the book up under my shirt. I glanced down the hall. Trey was gone. Had he seen Danny give me the book? If he did, the first thing he would do is run and tell his mom. I popped one of my braids in my mouth and sucked on it.

"Sorry," Danny said. "I thought you'd be excited."

"I am. Yeah. I'm sorry," I told him. I pulled the book out and put it quickly into my locker. It was one of the books off Mrs. Spencer's new list that I didn't have.

"Javy's older brother had a copy of it," Danny said. "He thinks he might have *Bridge to Terabithia* around somewhere too. He's going to look for it this weekend. I'll let you know."

I didn't understand why Danny was so into finding all the books on the list. He wasn't interested in reading them all like I was. I thanked him anyway and put the book in my locker. We had to get to class.

"Have you read any of the Wayside School books?" I asked him. "I think you'd like them. They're really funny."

Danny flicked his hair into place. "Cool. I didn't know you had those. I'll pick one up after school." We went into Mr. Vaughn's class, and he walked with me to my desk. Rebecca was already sitting in the desk beside mine.

"Hey, you've got so many books now you need a list," Danny whispered. "You know. To let everybody know what's in the B.B.L.L."

"I know, I know," I told him. "Nikoli said the same thing."

"Right. And what's she supposed to do, tape it to the front of her locker?" Rebecca said. "She gets caught, and it's lawsuit time."

I felt the quicksand opening up underneath me again. "Lawsuit time?"

"Sure. From all the parents whose children you've corrupted. Why do you think they banned all those books to begin with? Because the parents think they're going to rot our brains and turn us into violent criminals."

Danny ran his fingers through his hair. "I don't know about you guys, but ever since I read *Wait Till Helen Comes,* I've been thinking about worshiping Satan. He's got some really good ideas."

"Don't joke! This is serious," I said. "Is this serious, Rebecca?"

"Aw, come on," Danny said. "Nobody's gonna sue you. Suspend you, maybe, but not sue you."

"*Definitely* suspended," Rebecca agreed.

The quicksand turned into water, and I sank to the bottom, desk and all.

Juvenile Delinquents

All through math I sucked on my braids and imagined all the awful things that would happen if I was caught with all those books in my locker. Every parent at Shelbourne Elementary would line up to sue me. My dad would lose his bricklaying business. My mom would lose her job. We'd have to sell our house and move to a different city. My sisters would have to be sold to medical research companies.

Well, it wouldn't *all* be so bad.

I was overreacting, and I knew it. What I was doing wasn't exactly illegal. The school board had just said that *Mrs. Jones* couldn't loan out these books. They didn't say *I* couldn't.

I still wanted to loan out the books, but I didn't want to get caught.

So how was I going to let people know what books I had to check out? If I didn't have a way of telling the other kids what I had, they wouldn't know to ask for them, and nobody would read them. Then it would all be for nothing.

And then I had it. Why *not* tape a list of the books I had on my locker? I just didn't have to call it that! During language arts, I used one of the computers to type up a list, and I taped it to my locker after school. At the top, in big capital letters, it said, BOOKS BANNED AT SHELBOURNE ELEMENTARY. Underneath that was every one of the books Mrs. Spencer and the other parents had taken off the shelves, with a little dot from a green Magic Marker next to all the books I had in the B.B.L.L. Once everybody knew how to read it, I could just add a new green dot to any book that got added. Presto!

Looking at the list again, I realized there were still a lot of books I needed to add, and Danny was running out of people to ask. What I needed was money to buy books with.

"Bake sale," Rebecca said.

"Of course!" I said. A bake sale! Every time we wanted to raise money to help build a well in Africa or to support the Red Cross after a hurricane, we had a bake sale! All I had to do was tell my dad we were having another bake sale at school, and he picked up a brownie mix at the store without even asking what it was for. Same with Rebecca's mom.

Rebecca and I set up our plastic-wrapped brownies and chocolate-chip cookies in a basket on a table in the cafeteria and started raking in the moolah. The first day we made $7.50. I was counting out the quarters again when Rebecca nudged me.

"What?" I said.

Rebecca nudged me again, harder.

"What?" I said. I looked up and saw Principal Banana coming right for us.

Her name isn't Principal Banana, of course. It's Banazewski. But none of the kindergarteners could ever pronounce her name right, so she let them call her Principal Banana. As fourth graders, we were supposed to call her Principal Banazewski though.

Principal Banazewski reminded me of a police detective from one of those TV mysteries. She wore gray suits and black leather shoes, and she always had a walkie-talkie on her belt and her school ID in a plastic holder pinned to her jacket like a badge. I expected her to yell "Freeze, punk! You're under arrest!" every time I saw her.

Instead she looked over our selection of desserts and said, "Looks good, ladies. What's the cause?"

"The what?" I said.

"What are you raising money for?" Principal Banazewski asked. Her walkie-talkie squawked, and she turned down the volume on it without looking at it.

I pulled a braid around and chewed on it.

"Uh . . ." I said. I looked at Rebecca. Her eyes went wide and she shook her head.

"We, uh . . ." I stammered. We couldn't tell her what our bake sale was really for. I was going to have to make something up! What had our last bake sale been for? I couldn't remember. With Detective Banazewski staring at me, I couldn't think of anything!

"We're raising money for . . . books," I said.

"Books?" Principal Banazewski said.

Rebecca gawked at me.

"Books for . . . prisoners!" I said. "For them to read. In prison."

Rebecca closed her eyes. I think she might have been praying.

"Books for prisoners?" Principal Banazewski said.

"Kid prisoners. Kids our age who are in jail."

Under the table, Rebecca started hitting me in the leg with her fist.

"You mean, juvenile delinquents?" Principal Banazewski said.

"*Yes,*" I said. "Juvenile delinquents. We're raising money to buy books for juvenile delinquents." That sounded good.

"Well, that's very noble of you," Principal Banazewski said. "I'll take two cookies." She handed over a dollar, and I had to kick Rebecca to get her to open her eyes and take the money.

Rebecca turned on me the second Principal Banazewski was gone.

"'*Books for kid prisoners to read in jail*'?" she said.

"Well what was I supposed to say?" I said.

"We're raising money for the homeless! Or the animal shelter! Or the food bank!"

"Where were all these great ideas when she was asking!?" I said.

"Well, I thought you would think of something else besides, you know, *what we're actually raising money for*!" Rebecca said.

"Oh yeah?" I said. "Well, you just wait till Helen comes, and then you'll be sorry for picking on me!"

Rebecca and I busted out laughing.

"I'm sorry, all right?" I said. "Every time I see Principal Banana, I think of the police. It makes me nervous."

"Well, at least you didn't lie to her," Rebecca said. "We *are* raising money to buy books for juvenile delinquents: us."

Helen Comes

There was another school board meeting the next month. I didn't go, but I knew what happened. Mrs. Jones argued again that none of the books should be removed from the library, but the school board still agreed with Mrs. Spencer. All the books from her second list were officially banned.

The very next day in social studies, Mr. Vaughn told us we were going to start studying the Bill of Rights.

The Founding Fathers wrote the Constitution to explain how the new American government would work, but then they realized they needed an extra part to talk about all the freedoms Americans automatically got that the government couldn't take away from them. That's what the Bill of Rights is. It's ten amendments that protect the natural rights of all citizens.

"The Constitution was important because it told the world how we were going to run our government," Mr. Vaughn said. "The Bill of Rights might be even more important though, because it said what our new country was going to be about. It said, 'Here are the rights we think are so important that no one can take them away from us, not even the government.' We added a lot more later on, but the first ten are very famous. It was the first document of its kind in the world.

"For this social studies unit I'm going to split you up into pairs," Mr. Vaughn told us. "Each team will study a different amendment. Your assignment will be to give a presentation to the class that explains what your amendment means. How you do that—what kind of presentation you give—is up to you."

Rebecca's hand shot up. "Mr. Vaughn! Can I do the Sixth Amendment? *Please?*"

"Um, sure, Rebecca," Mr. Vaughn said. He erased something in his notes and wrote in something new.

I looked at Rebecca like she was crazy.

"The Sixth Amendment is the right to a trial by jury," she told me. "And the right to counsel."

"Does . . . anyone else have a favorite amendment they want to do?" Mr. Vaughn asked.

Not surprisingly, no one else did.

"All right," Mr. Vaughn said. "Janna, I want you and Traci to take the Fifth Amendment. Kevin, you and Danny take the Second Amendment . . ."

I tuned out while Mr. Vaughn gave the other assignments. Rebecca and I had made another seven dollars in our most recent bake sale, and I was trying to decide whether to buy *How to Eat Fried Worms* or Anne Frank's *The Diary of a Young Girl*. They were really hard to compare.

"Amy Anne?" Mr. Vaughn said. "Are you with us?"

"Sorry," I said. Beside me, I could sense Rebecca's eyes boring into me, but I focused on Mr. Vaughn.

"I said I'm assigning you and Trey the First Amendment. That all right?"

Was that all right? Was I all right with working on my social studies project with the son of my archenemy? The boy who would rat me out the second I slipped up and mentioned the B.B.L.L.? No, I was definitely *not* all right with that.

But instead I said, "Okay."

"All right. Everybody get together with your partner and start reading about your amendment," Mr. Vaughn said. "I'll be coming around to help."

Everybody else got up and put their desks together. I sat where I was and made Trey drag his desk all the way across the room to me. He parked it right up against mine with a thud, making my pencil pop out of its little ditch.

Trey stared at his closed notebook. I crossed my arms and stared at my textbook.

"You don't like me much, do you?" Trey asked.

I wanted to laugh. "Don't like you much?" I wanted to say. "Oh, why would that be, Trey? Maybe because besides your mom banning my favorite book, you drew that awful picture of me last year!"

Trey likes to draw. That's his thing. And I hated to admit it, but he was really good. He was so good that last year, when Trey and I were both in Mrs. Maples's room, he decided he would draw each of us as animals. Mrs. Maples was a wise old maple tree. Kenny Haskins, who was good at soccer, he drew as a cheetah. Lavina Maddox, who wanted to be a singer when she grew up, he drew as a songbird. Daniel Farid, who loved the Teenage Mutant Ninja Turtles, he drew as a ninja turtle. Everybody loved the pictures he drew of them.

Except me.

The picture Trey drew of Amy Anne Ollinger was a mouse sitting on a book, chewing its tail. He didn't draw me as a cheetah or a ninja turtle or a songbird. He drew me as a wimpy little mouse!

Trey bent his head down to look up at me, and I realized I hadn't said anything for a long time.

"Listen, Amy Anne—" he said at last.

The room intercom crackled to life, making both of us jump.

"Mr. Vaughn?" the secretary said. "I'm sorry for the interruption. But can we please see Jeffrey Gonzalez and Amy Anne Ollinger in the office?"

"Ooooooooooh," the rest of the class said. Everybody always did that anytime anybody got called to the office, like you were in big trouble, even if it was just because you had a dentist appointment. But this time, they knew they might be right. Half the eyes in the room were on me, and I knew why. They all knew I ran the B.B.L.L., and they were all thinking the exact same thing I was:

Amy Anne is busted.

"I'll send them right along, Mrs. Perry," Mr. Vaughn said, motioning at the same time for us to get a move on.

My legs felt like Jell-O as I stood. Across the room, Rebecca's and Danny's faces looked like they had just seen Helen's ghost by the pond. I didn't know how I was even going to walk to the door without collapsing.

I put my hand on Trey's desk to steady myself, and he looked up at me.

"Hope you're not in trouble," he said.

The Banana Room

 Hope you're not in trouble.

That rat fink Trey! He knew I was in trouble because he was the one who ratted me out! *Hope you're not in trouble.* Ha. Very funny, Trey.

I was right where he wanted me to be, walking the Long March of Death with Jeffrey Gonzalez to the principal's office. I sucked on my braids. The more I thought about it, the madder I got at Trey.

"So what if I have a bunch of banned books in my locker? I'm not breaking any rules, Trey!" That's what I should have said to him. "Just because *your mom* took them out of the library doesn't mean I have to take them out of my locker!"

"I didn't do anything wrong," Jeffrey said. I jumped a little, surprised to hear him say what I was thinking. He clearly thought he was in big trouble too. What he'd been called to the office for, I had no idea. Jeffrey was a small, round, Mexican kid with short, spiky hair and Harry

Potter glasses. He was quiet, like me, but he was quiet because his brain was always somewhere else. The only time you could ever really get him talking was when you asked him about the science-fiction movies he liked. In second grade, Lena Harvey had called him Space Cadet, and the nickname stuck.

"I can't have done anything wrong," Jeffrey said. "At least, I don't think so. Did you do anything?"

I guess not everybody had heard about the Banned Books Locker Library. If he had, he would have known exactly why I was being called to the office. We turned the corner of the fourth grade hall. The office was just a few steps away. As soon as I saw it, all my anger was gone. Rebecca's words came back to me then: *"Definitely suspended."*

I didn't want to get suspended! I couldn't get suspended. No kid had gotten suspended in the whole time I'd been at Shelbourne Elementary. Getting suspended was something that happened to only really bad kids. The serious troublemakers. Kids who were going to grow up to become people who chained dogs up in their front yard and threw trash out their car window.

Jeffrey and I went into the office. The secretary, Mrs. Perry, told Jeffrey that Principal Banazewski would see him first, and told me to sit and wait. Jeffrey swallowed, gave me a "wish me luck" glance, and went into the principal's office. The door closed behind him.

I sat in one of the chairs outside Detective Banazewski's office like a criminal waiting to go into the interrogation room. But I wasn't a criminal! I never did anything to get in trouble. I never did anything, period.

But that wasn't true, was it? I was here because I *had* done something. For some reason I had decided to get as many of the books Mrs. Spencer had banned from the library and loan them out to as many people in my class as I could. Why had I done that? Why did I care? What did it matter if Mrs. Spencer banned those books? My parents would buy me whatever books I really wanted to read. I sucked on my braids and wondered what had gotten into me. This is why I kept quiet and never did anything. People who said and did whatever they were thinking got into trouble.

Principal Banazewski's door opened, and she led Jeffrey out. He looked stunned, like someone had told him there wasn't really such a thing as aliens.

"I'm sure your grandmother was a terrific person, Jeffrey," Mrs. Banazewski said, "and I know you'll miss her very much. Go ahead and collect your things, and you can wait here until your parents come."

Jeffrey nodded, just barely, and left the office without even looking at me.

"Miss Ollinger?" Principal Banazewski said, gesturing for me to join her in her office.

Any doubt I might have had about why I was called

to the office was officially gone. No adult ever called you by your last name unless you were in deep, deep trouble.

I stepped through into Principal Banazewski's office. I'd never been in here before. It was a square little room with white cinder block walls and no windows. I thought there might be one of those big mirrors they have in interrogation rooms, where people on the other side can see through, but the only things on the walls were lots of framed certificates and plaques with her name on them, pictures of her family, and bananas.

Lots and lots of bananas.

There were bananas everywhere. Banana paintings, bananas with arms and legs and faces, monkeys with bananas, banana hats, banana slippers, Banana Republic ads, a collection of those blue stickers that come on bananas—basically anything and everything that said or showed a banana on it. I guess kindergarteners had been giving her banana stuff forever.

Principal Banazewski told me to sit, and sat down behind her banana-decorated desk. "Miss Ollinger, we need to talk about your locker," she said.

"I'm sorry! I'm so sorry! I didn't mean to do anything bad. I just hated it so much that Mrs. Spencer took away my favorite book. At first, all I was going to do was just read all the books she banned, but then I started collecting them, and other people wanted to read them. It wasn't anybody's fault but mine! I swear, I'll take them home and never ever bring another one to school again. Just don't suspend me!"

That's what I wanted to say. But I was so scared all I said was, "My locker?"

Principal Banazewski leaned forward. "Yes. Specifically, the piece of paper you have taped to the outside of your locker."

I blinked. "The piece of paper?"

"The one that says BOOKS BANNED AT SHELBOURNE ELEMENTARY."

The list of banned books I put on my locker? Why was she talking about that? The books inside were the big deal. I felt a little hiccup of hope. Was the list all this was about? Or did Mrs. Banazewski know *why* I put that list on my locker? I stared at a grinning banana with sunglasses on her desk and hoped she didn't know about the stack of banned books inside my locker.

"First," Principal Banazewski said, "I don't like the word 'banned.' Those books weren't banned from the library. They were removed from the library."

"What's the difference?" I asked.

I threw a hand over my mouth. Had I said that out loud? What was I thinking?

Principal Banazewski's voice got that *you-don't-know-anything* tone adults get when they don't like being questioned. "The difference," Mrs. Banazewski said, "is that in one case, books are banned arbitrarily. Do you know what arbitrarily means?"

"For no good reason?"

"In a way, yes. It can also mean based on just one person's opinion, not the opinion of others. In this case, the books weren't removed arbitrarily. They were inappropriate, and more than one person agreed that was true. A whole school board, in fact. So they were removed."

"But it *was* just one person—Mrs. Spencer," I wanted to say. "She didn't like one book, and she got the school board to ban it. Then she helped other people who didn't like other books do the same thing, when there might be lots more people out there who *do* like them. Or just don't care."

But this time I didn't say anything. Blurting out an objection was one thing; arguing with the principal was another. Still, I didn't see what the difference between banning and removing was. Either way, kids couldn't read them.

And that's when I remembered why I started the B.B.L.L. in the first place. *Good books shouldn't be hidden away. They should be read by as many people as many times as possible.* But that wasn't exactly true. It wasn't just *good* books that shouldn't be hidden away. It was *all* books. Any books. It didn't matter what they were about, or whether I liked them, or Mrs. Spencer liked them, or the school board liked them.

I was lucky. My parents would buy me any book I wanted if I asked them to. But not everybody's parents would do that. Not everybody's parents *could* do that. That's what libraries were for: to make sure that everybody had the same access to the same books everyone else did. That's why I started the Banned Books Locker Library, and that was why I was going to get every last book Mrs. Spencer had banned. Even Captain Underpants.

"I think it's the same thing," I said. Out loud. My voice got a little shaky as I spoke, but I kept going. "Banning and removing. Either way, people can't read them. And that's all that really matters."

Principal Banazewski took a deep breath. "Regardless," she said, "the school board is the ultimate authority here, and they've made their decision and the books have been removed. There's no reason to go advertising it."

"If there's nothing wrong with it, why do you care if anybody finds out?" I wanted to ask her. I didn't say it though. I'd said enough already. But as I thought it, I realized I could be asking myself the same question. If there was nothing wrong with the B.B.L.L., why was I keeping it a secret? I blushed, feeling guilty about the B.B.L.L. all over again.

"So," Principal Banazewski said, "you'll take it down by the end of the period."

It wasn't a question.

B.B.L.L. Inc.

I took down the list of banned books by the end of the period.

In its place, I hung up a construction paper sign I'd drawn that said, GO EAGLES! #1!

The Eagles were the Shelbourne Elementary mascot.

Principal Banazewski would be happy to see my sign. She likes school spirit. She would not be happy to see what was on the back of it. That's where I taped my old banned books list. If you flipped up the GO EAGLES! #1 sign, the list was right there.

After all, I still had to have some way to let people know what books I had.

I wanted more books for the B.B.L.L. though. I wanted all the books Mrs. Spencer had banned. I wanted a giant tower of books that filled my locker. And I wanted everyone to read them.

Rebecca said that to do all that, we needed to incorporate.

"I hereby call to order the first meeting of the B.B.L.L. Board of Trustees," she announced officially, even though it was just me and Danny sitting with her at one end of a table in the cafeteria. She had an extra-long pad to take notes on, which she used only because it was called a legal pad. "Present are Rebecca Zimmerman, Esquire; Danny Purcell; and Amy Anne Ollinger."

I liked how I came last, even though I was the one who started the B.B.L.L.

"Do we really need to do this?" I asked.

"We do if this corporation wants to grow," Rebecca said. "First, we need to elect officers. I nominate myself as chief financial officer and legal counsel."

Danny and I stared at her.

Danny shrugged. "Okay."

"You're supposed to say, 'Second' if you agree," Rebecca said.

"Second," Danny and I said.

Rebecca huffed. "You're not both supposed to say it. Just one of you. Then I say, 'All in favor?'"

Danny and I looked at each other.

"Me?" Danny said.

"You're supposed to say, 'Aye,'" Rebecca said.

"Eye like eye?" Danny said, pointing to where his eyes would have been if hair wasn't covering them.

"Aye like 'A-Y-E,'" Rebecca said. "It means yes."

"Then why don't we just say yes?" I asked.

Rebecca looked like she was going to explode, so Danny jumped in. "Aye then! Aye," he said quickly.

Rebecca looked at me.

"What?" I asked.

"Well? Aren't you going to vote?"

"I thought only one of us was supposed to say it!"

"That's when you second something!" Rebecca said. "When I say 'All in favor,' everyone votes 'aye' or 'nay.'"

"Can we just skip all that?" I asked. "You're the one in charge of money."

Rebecca sagged, and I felt bad. She just wanted to play at being a lawyer, I knew, but if she kept this up we'd be here for the rest of lunch period and never get anything done.

Danny flicked his hair into place. "So what do I get to be?"

"You're in charge of alternative acquisitions," Rebecca said. "That means getting the books that we can't afford to buy."

"Sweet," Danny said. "I've got some ideas about that. So far, I've only been asking fourth graders and their brothers and sisters. But I know some kids in third grade, and in fifth grade. If I put the word out, I'll bet I can dig up a lot more books."

"Just don't put the word out too much!" I said. I'd already told them both about my meeting with Principal Banana. The only reason I was still living and breathing was because she hadn't found out about the Banned Books Locker Library.

"You want people to check out the books, don't you?" Danny asked.

"Of course. Just don't go hanging signs for the B.B.L.L. in the hallway."

Rebecca finished writing Danny's title down. "All right. That leaves Amy Anne."

"What's she?" Danny asked.

"President and chief librarian," Rebecca said.

President and chief librarian! I liked that. Even though we'd been calling the Locker Library a *library,* I hadn't thought of myself as a librarian. Just the person with the locker. I didn't know anything about being a librarian, except for what I'd seen Mrs. Jones do, and I said so.

"Well, you're going to have to learn," Rebecca said. "And the first thing you're going to have to figure out is how to keep track of how long people have the books."

Danny ran his fingers through his hair. "Yeah! I've been waiting forever to read that Shel Silverstein book, but T.J. still has it!"

"I don't want to have due dates and library fines and all that," I said.

"Well, you need to consider it. At least due dates. Or some of the books are never going to come back again."

Rebecca and Danny went on talking about more bake sales, and which books he thought he might be able to get, but I was still thinking about a better way of keeping track of who had what book, and how long they'd had it. The clipboard with the list in my locker was getting to be lots of pages long, and every time I got a book back in I had to skim through all the names and holds to find out who wanted the book next. The B.B.L.L. was getting too big for its britches, as my grandmother liked to say. I was going to have to figure out a better system, and there was only one person I knew to ask.

Tools of the Trade

I stopped at the library's front desk before heading for my spot in the corner after school. I watched as a second grader checked out a small stack of books. Mrs. Jones scanned the little bar codes on the back with her laser thing, and the computer recorded what book it was the kid was checking out, and when it was due back. That was no help. I didn't have a computer, or a scanner, or whatever program she had that kept track of it all.

Mrs. Jones noticed me watching. "Thinking of becoming a librarian, Amy Anne?" she asked.

I jumped. People were always reading my mind! "What? Oh. No! I was just interested in how it all worked. You know, the way you keep track of what books get checked out."

Mrs. Jones ran the boy's books across the bonky thing that made them safe to take through the detectors at the front door without setting off the alarm. "It's all automated now," Mrs. Jones said. "Certainly a lot less trouble than it used to be."

"What did it used to be like?" I asked her.

"Let's see," Mrs. Jones said. She looked over at the paperback spinner racks. "Bring me that copy of *The Witch of Blackbird Pond*."

It was an old, beat-up copy of the book, with clear cellophane tape holding the covers on. Mrs. Jones flipped to the back of the book.

"Ah. I thought this one might still have it in there! We've gone all digital now, of course, but I never got around to taking these out of the older books." She turned the book around for me to see.

There, in the back cover, was a little manila envelope with a card sticking out of it. Mrs. Jones pulled out the card.

"It's a date due card," she explained. "Used to be, we would have to take the card out of every book, stamp it with the due date, and then the person checking the book out would sign the card."

Of course! I had seen these in the back of some of the books I checked out, but never paid much attention to them. The card had the book's name and author at the top. Underneath that were two columns—one for the date, and another for the borrower's name. The dates in the book were all from the 1980s. The names on this date due card had to be adults by now.

"They took the books, and we kept the card," Mrs. Jones said. "We put the cards in order by the date, and then every day we would check to see what books had come due."

"How did the person checking the books out know when they were due?" I asked her.

"Oh. We put a little slip of paper in each little pocket in the back, with the due date stamped on it. The whole thing was an absolute headache for a large library."

I was excited. My library was tiny. This was exactly what I needed!

"Do you have a different stamp for every day?"

"Oh heavens, no. There was a neat little gizmo that could stamp any date. I wonder if I still have one."

Mrs. Jones disappeared into the back office. I could see her rummaging around in a drawer through the windows.

Envelopes. I could use a bunch of envelopes, and tape them into the backs of the B.B.L.L. books. Then I could stick index cards down inside the little pockets, with places for people to sign their names! When the books were due, I could even slip a reminder notice into the borrower's locker mailbox.

"Aha! Found one!" Mrs. Jones said. "Just goes to show you, we never throw anything away around here." She came back with a complicated little hand stamp that was stained red from years of use. It had a black knob on the top where you held it, and on the bottom were four rotating rubber pieces—one for the month, two for the numbers in the date, and one for the year. It was set for May 27, 1988.

Mrs. Jones laughed. "I suppose that was the last day we ever used it."

I clicked the month forward and back. What an awesome gadget! I tried stamping it on my arm, but it was dry, of course. It only left a faint imprint of the date on my skin.

"Where can I get one of these?" I asked.

Mrs. Jones looked surprised. "Oh. Well, I suppose they still sell them somewhere. Office supply stores, maybe? Though I don't know how much call there is for them today. You can have that one, if you want it."

The little hairs on my arms tingled. "Really?"

"Well, I certainly don't need it anymore," Mrs. Jones said. "And it is a little out of date. It only has the years 1980 to 1990 on it."

I didn't care. The date due stamp was too amazing. I would make it work somehow. "Thanks!" I said, and I ran off to my corner.

All I needed now was a pair of glasses on a chain, and I was ready for my official librarian membership card.

Nowhere to Stomp To

The index cards and envelopes I found in my mom's home office, which doubled as the treadmill room, and tripled as the guest bedroom, and quadrupled as the place where we dumped all the holiday stuff and anything else we didn't have a place for. Angelina's room had a glue stick, and there was a pair of scissors in the kitchen drawer. Now all I needed was a place to work.

My bed wasn't a great place to cut and paste. Alexis was in there using my bedpost for a ballet barre again and playing her music too loud. The kitchen table would have been perfect, but Angelina had turned it into a pony barn. She'd used the paper shredder in mom's office to make hay again, and it was scattered all over the floor. I went to the living room instead, where Mom and Dad were watching something with knights and swords on TV.

Dad paused the show they were watching as I came in. "What's up, kiddo?"

"Just school stuff," I said. I set my things down on the coffee table and settled in.

"Oh—I'm sorry, hon. We need you to find someplace else to work tonight," Mom said. "We're watching something you're not old enough to watch yet."

"And where do you expect me to go?" I wanted to ask them. "Alexis has turned my room into a ballet studio, and Angelina has turned the kitchen into a stable!"

I sighed heavily instead. I snatched up my things as angrily as I could and stomped into the kitchen.

"I need the kitchen table," I told Angelina.

"Neigh," she said.

I plunked my things down on the table.

"You're just playing. I have a school project to do," I told her.

"Neigh!" Angelina said.

I pulled out a chair and sat down, messing up her piles of shredded paper.

"No! *No!* I was here first! I was here first!" Angelina screamed. She grabbed the chair I was sitting in and yanked on it. When she couldn't move it, she tried pulling me by the arm out of the chair.

"Let go! I'm working!"

"You're ruining it! You're ruining it!"

"Angelina! Amy Anne!" my father called from the living room. "Enough!"

Angelina stopped trying to pull me out of the chair and collapsed onto the floor, where she rolled around kicking her legs and screaming at the top of her lungs.

"Girls!" Dad bellowed from the living room. "I do not want to deal with this right now!"

"I was here first!" Angelina wailed. *"I was here first!"*

"Amy Anne," Mom called. "Your sister was already using the kitchen. Find someplace else to work!"

I pushed my chair back from the table with as much noise as I could, picked up my things, and stomped out of the kitchen, kicking Angelina's piles of shredded paper into the air as I went. She wailed even louder, which made me feel good even though I was steaming mad.

I still needed somewhere to work. I wasn't going to fight another battle with Alexis in my room. Not after Angelina had already gotten my parents angry. And I needed more room than my old hideout, the bathroom. Angelina's fit and my parents yelling at us had woken the dogs and sent them scurrying into the hall, nubby tails down and unhappy. They didn't like it when we yelled, and they were looking for a place to hide like I was.

Flotsam and Jetsam followed me into Mom's office. The bed was covered with boxes of Christmas decorations and blankets and camping gear we had never used, and Mom's desk was piled so high with papers and folders and boxes that it was useless. There was room on the floor though. I plopped down with as much frustration as I could and spread out my envelopes and note cards.

Which Flotsam and Jetsam proceeded to step all over.

"No! No!" I told them, but they kept moving around, their tails wiggling in happiness as they bent my cards and envelopes. They weren't trying to be bad. They were just trying to get as close to me as possible, and since I was on the floor they thought I was down there to pet them and play with them.

I dodged the dogs' big legs and collected all my things again and pushed past them into the hall. There wasn't a single place in this house I could work. I stomped through the kitchen again, where Angelina eyed me warily from underneath the table. I didn't even bother kicking her shredded paper. I went straight to the back door and outside.

Where it was raining.

I dashed to Mom's car and jumped into the front passenger seat. There was no flat space to glue, and the car still smelled like sour milk, but at least I could work there in peace. If only I could drive—then I would have started the car and driven far, far away from there.

I ran the back of my arm across my eyes, and I couldn't tell if I was wiping away rain or tears.

The Right to Bear Arms

Trey had already pulled our desks together when I got to class the next day. It was time to work on our Bill of Rights project together. Not that I expected him to do any of the actual work. All he did in class was draw pictures.

I heaved my swelling backpack up onto my desk with a *thunk*.

"Whoa," Trey said. "What have you got, like every schoolbook you own in there?"

"Yes," I said. I unzipped my bag and pulled my social studies textbook out from the rest. It hit my desk with another *thunk*. "It's very heavy."

"Why don't you keep all your books in your locker?" Trey asked.

I froze. Stupid, Amy Anne! Stupid! The reason I had all my textbooks stuffed in my backpack was because all the space in my locker was taken up by banned books, but of course I couldn't tell Trey that.

"I hate having to go out to my locker," I lied.

"But I see you out at your locker all the time," Trey said. "You're always meeting people there."

He was on to me. There was no question. He was trying to catch me in a lie, but I wasn't going to fall for it.

"Can we just get to our project?" I said. "We missed a whole day because I had to go to the office." I dug in my stuffed backpack for the notes I'd made on the First Amendment.

Trey pulled out the sketchbook he carried everywhere. "Yeah. What happened? Did you get in trouble with Principal Banana?"

"No," I told him. I looked him in the eyes. Had he expected me to get in trouble? Was he just messing with me? If he was, he was hiding it pretty well.

"That's good," he said, but I didn't believe him.

"Here are my notes on the First Amendment," I said.

"Cool," he said. "I drew some pictures."

"Of what?" I asked. *More pictures of me as a mouse?*

Trey looked confused. "Um, the Bill of Rights. For our project."

I was stunned. Trey had actually done work on our project? He turned his sketchbook around so I could see. It was a drawing of a man with huge, furry arms with claws at the end. I frowned.

"What's this?" I asked.

"The right to bear arms," he said.

I rolled my eyes. "It's bear like *carry*, not bear like *bear*," I said. "And besides, that's the Second Amendment. We're doing the First Amendment."

"I know," he said with a little smile. "I couldn't help it. It was too funny."

It was the first time I had ever seen Trey smile, and it surprised me. He had a really friendly face under his uncombed blond hair when he smiled. For a second I kind of liked him and his funny drawing, which really was pretty good. But then I remembered who he was and what he'd done to me in third grade.

"What does MMIII mean?" I asked. It was written in the bottom corner of the picture. "Is that Roman numerals or something?"

"That's my signature," Trey said. "Marvin McBride III."

"Marvin McBride? I thought your name was Trey Spencer," I said.

"Trey is just my nickname. And my mom and dad divorced when I was in kindergarten, and they both remarried," he said. "McBride is my dad's last name. He's a commercial illustrator. He lives in Atlanta with his new family. My mom married a guy whose last name is Wheeler, but she'd already gone back to using Spencer. That's her maiden name."

"Oh," I said. I didn't know what else to say to that. "Did you . . . do anything on the First Amendment?"

"Yeah," Trey said. He flipped to another page, where he'd drawn a picture of people bowing down before a weird-looking alien coming out of a UFO.

"Um, what is this?" I asked.

"They're worshiping an alien, see? The First Amendment says Congress can't make laws about establishing religions, so they're free to worship aliens if they want."

"I . . . don't think that's exactly what it's saying. That part is about how the government can't establish one religion and make everybody follow it."

"Oh," Trey said. He turned his picture around and looked at it. "Too bad. I really liked that alien."

"It works for the other part about religion," I told him. "The free exercise clause. That's the one that says the government can't stop you from believing in whatever religion you want. What did you draw for that one?"

Trey flipped to the next page. In that picture, a bunch of people in pope hats and robes were lifting weights.

"Um . . ." I said. I had no idea what I was looking at.

"The free exercise of religion," Trey said. He smiled slyly again. He knew that the free exercise of religion really meant you could worship whoever you wanted to, however you wanted to, not people in church doing weightlifting. But it *was* funny. I smiled despite myself.

"I think we better use the UFO picture instead of that one," I told him.

"Yeah," he said. "Oh! I've got another one for freedom of the press."

The picture showed a woman pressing the middle of three big buttons.

"See?" Trey said. "She's got the freedom to press whichever button she wants!"

I snorted, then caught myself. I did not want to like Trey or his pictures.

"You do know that freedom of the press means you can print anything you want, and the government can't tell you not to, right?"

Trey shrugged. "Mine's funnier."

"Did you do anything for the freedom to assemble?"

Trey turned the page to a picture of a boy sitting on the floor building with Legos. I closed my eyes and shook my head.

"I thought about having him assemble a model car, but more people would get the Lego thing," he said.

"The right to assembly says—"

"That we can get together in public and protest stuff if we want," Trey said. "I know, I know. I drew a real one for the right to petition. I couldn't think of anything funny for that."

His picture of the right to petition showed a clipboard with lots of signatures on it. So there were at least two usable pictures. I ran down my list of the rights protected in the First Amendment. There was only one we hadn't done. The right to free speech. Trey said he had a picture for that one too, and he flipped through his sketchbook looking for it.

I expected Trey to have drawn a picture of somebody giving a speech without charging for it, or maybe a speech bubble or the word SPEECH breaking out of jail and going free. Instead what he showed me was a drawing of a locker with a sign on it that said, BOOKS BANNED AT SHELBOURNE ELEMENTARY.

My locker.

I looked up at Trey in surprise. He wasn't smiling this time, or even looking at me. He was staring at his hands. He was right though. Making me take down my sign was against the freedom of speech. I hadn't even thought of it that way.

But had he drawn it because he agreed with me, or disagreed with me? I frowned at the thought.

"Are you ever going to tell me why you don't like me?" Trey asked.

"You shouldn't have to ask!" I wanted to yell. "You should know that your mom is an awful person for banning books and *you're* an awful person for spying on me and drawing that stupid picture of me last year!"

Instead I just grabbed the edges of my chair and stared angrily at my desk.

Mr. Vaughn announced that it was time to put away our social studies and get out our vocab books.

"Okay. Well, I'll work on the others and show them to you when I'm done," Trey said, and he dragged his desk back across to the other side of the room.

And, in this corner . . .

I kept trying to focus on *Liar & Spy* in my spot in the corner of the library, but all I could think about was Trey. He'd seen my list of banned books on my locker, and studied it enough to draw it—and get all the books right on the list. That meant he had to know it had been taken down too. I thought he would have wanted that. But the way he acted when he showed me the picture . . . it was like he was embarrassed. Or sorry.

"Hey," Trey said.

I jumped, spitting out the braid I was sucking on. I was just thinking about him, and there he was, standing next to me!

"Sorry," he said. "I didn't mean to scare you. I just—I drew a new picture of the right to assemble, and I wanted to show it to you before I went home."

Trey showed me. He'd drawn it right this time. The picture was of a bunch of people standing on a sidewalk with signs in their hands that all said VOTE NO! All but one. It said MAGNETS: HOW DO THEY WORK!?

" 'Magnets: How do they work'?" I asked him.

"How *do* they work? It's like magic!" he said. His smile told me he was joking. "Anyway, that guy has as much right to be there as the rest of them, right?"

"Yeah," I said. "Only that's not the freedom of assembly. That's the freedom of speech."

"Yeah," Trey said. He looked at the floor again.

"The rest of it works though," I said. "And you draw really great. All the faces are different. And you even drew the hands." Any time I had to draw a person, I drew her with her hands behind her back, or stuck in her pockets. Because I couldn't draw hands and fingers.

Trey shrugged. "If you want to draw comic books, you have to be able to draw hands."

I was about to ask Trey if that's what he wanted to do, draw comic books, when we both heard his mother's voice there in the library.

"Good afternoon, Mrs. Jones," Mrs. Spencer said.

"Mrs. Spencer," Mrs. Jones said.

Mrs. Jones was wearing a wide green dress with white polka dots. Mrs. Spencer was wearing a tiny powder-blue track suit. They looked like the illustrations for big and little in a picture book, and they stood staring at each other like those two Dr. Seuss characters who won't get out of each other's way while people build interstates around them.

"Is Trey in the library?" Mrs. Spencer asked finally.

"I think he's in the back," Mrs. Jones said. She nodded down the aisle to us, and my heart beat faster. It was dumb. Mrs. Spencer didn't know who I was, or what I was doing with her list of banned books. But I was still so nervous I stuck one of my braids in my mouth and sucked on it.

"Trey, it's time to go," Mrs. Spencer called.

"I guess my ride's here," Trey said. "See you."

Mrs. Spencer put her hand on Trey's head and was leading him out of the library when Mrs. Jones stopped them.

"Oh, Mrs. Spencer, I meant to thank you," she said.

Mrs. Spencer turned. "Thank me?"

"For the money you and the PTA raised to bring an author to the school. I just booked someone to visit—Dav Pilkey."

Mrs. Spencer frowned, trying to place the name. "Didn't he write . . ."

"The Captain Underpants books. Yes," Mrs. Jones said. *That you banned,* she could have said. But she didn't have to, because we all knew it.

Mrs. Spencer darkened. "Do you really think that's such a good idea right now?" she asked.

"I think it's a *great* idea right now," Mrs. Jones said.

Mrs. Spencer looked so small and so mad that I half expected her to say, "Oh yeah? Well you just wait till Helen comes! Then you'll be sorry!" Instead she turned and led Trey out of the library, her chest heaving in her track suit almost as much as if she'd actually exercised in it.

Round three in the boxing match had gone to Mrs. Jones. Maybe this fight wasn't over yet.

Helen Comes Again

Wait Till Helen Comes sat in the middle of the cafeteria floor, where everyone could see it.

Coletrane Farmer had been carrying it in secret, under his tray, when he ran into Orlando Choi, who was horsing around with Steve Rosales. Coletrane was a white second grader with sandy brown hair that laid flat on his head like a Roman general from my history book. He was currently obsessed with rock collecting, and when his tray went flying it sent mac and cheese, chocolate milk, and a dozen minerals of various shapes, sizes, and colors clattering and splattering all over the floor.

Along with *Wait Till Helen Comes*.

The kids in the cafeteria were still clapping and cheering for him, but I could barely hear them, or notice the splattered food and scattered rocks. Even the gross wet rag smell of the tables went away. It was like the only thing in the room for me at that moment was that book, laying right there out in the open like a spotlight was on it.

"All right, all right, that's enough," Principal Banaze-wski told everybody.

Principal Banazewski.

"Let me help you," Principal Banazewski told Cole-trane, and she bent over to pick up the book.

In five seconds, Detective Banazewski was going to pick up Prosecution Exhibit A in the case of *The Wake County School Board v. Amy Anne Ollinger,* and there wasn't a thing I could do about it but sit and watch.

"That's my seat!" someone across the room yelled. "I was sitting there!"

"Sit on this!" someone else yelled.

Two boys tumbled to the floor, kicking and pulling and punching. Just as quickly as they had cheered for Coletrane, the students in the cafeteria started chanting, *"Fight! Fight! Fight!"* I couldn't see who it was. They were just a tangle of arms and legs before kids fell into a circle around them to watch.

Principal Banazewski stood up, handed the book to Coletrane without even looking at it, and ran for the fight. "Break it up! Break it up!" she cried.

I hurried over to Coletrane. He had picked up his empty chocolate milk carton and was pretending to drink from it. "Ah," he said. *"Refreshing."*

"Go hide that in your locker," I whispered to him.

He looked at the chocolate milk carton. "What, this?"

"No! The book!"

He looked at the book in his hands and his eyes went wide as he understood.

"Oh, gosh! Sorry!" he said.

"Just hurry!" I told him. "And don't bring it to read in the cafeteria again!"

Coletrane hurried off. I went back to my seat and put my head on the table. That had been so close! Coletrane would have gotten in trouble, and then he would have to tell them where he got the book. The Locker Library was going great, but that meant that there were a lot of banned books out there in the hands of Shelbourne Elementary students. It was only a matter of time until another one of them slipped up and got caught with a book.

Danny and Rebecca sat down next to me as the teachers sent everyone back to their seats.

"Was that *Wait Till Helen Comes*?" Rebecca asked.

"Yes," I told her. "And Principal Banazewski had it *in her hands*."

"Lucky thing there was a fight," Danny said. He combed his hair away from his eyes. "Anybody see who it was?"

We all got an answer at the same time. The crowd cleared, and Principal Banazewski and Ms. Green each emerged with a different boy in hand. One of them I'd seen in the fourth grade hall, but didn't know. The other one was Jeffrey Gonzalez.

"That was my seat!" Jeffrey yelled. He lunged for the other boy again, but Principal Banazewski held him back.

"That's enough!" Principal Banazewski said. "We're all going to my office."

This time there was no fake oohing from the students. This was real, big-time trouble, and they knew it. As soon as they were gone, the cafeteria exploded with the excited chatter of everyone reliving every detail of the fight.

As bad as it was for Jeffrey, it had been a lucky thing the fight started when it did. Or maybe it wasn't lucky. Maybe Jeffrey had seen the book on the floor and started the fight as a distraction. But did Jeffrey even know about the B.B.L.L.? He hadn't that day we'd walked to the office together. If he'd done it on purpose, it was quick thinking. If he hadn't, it was just perfect timing for me. Either way, Jeffrey was going to be in big trouble, and either way, I owed him a big thank-you.

What's in a Name?

I couldn't thank Jeffrey Gonzalez the next day, because he got suspended for fighting.

Jeffrey was the first kid anyone could ever remember getting suspended for anything at Shelbourne Elementary. I hated the way people were whispering about him in the halls and in the cafeteria, like they enjoyed that somebody had gotten into big trouble. Like Jeffrey was some kind of awful criminal. Space Cadet was a geek, but he was a really nice guy. At least, he always had been.

"So, I've been thinking about our visibility problem," Danny said. I hadn't even seen him come sit at the desk next to me and Rebecca.

"Our visibility problem?" Rebecca said.

"As in, our books being visible when somebody drops one in the cafeteria?" I interpreted.

"Exactamundo." Danny flicked his hair back. "And I've got an idea. But it may require adding a new board member."

"Who?" I asked.

"Let's get passes to the computer lab and I'll introduce you," Danny said.

The computer lab had enough computers and printers for an entire class to use, but it was usually open for kids with passes unless a teacher had reserved it. Mr. Deacon checked our passes, and Danny led us to the back corner, where another kid was sitting. I'd never seen him before, which made me think he wasn't a fourth grader. But he looked like a fourth grader. Maybe even a third grader. He was short and stick thin, with skin as dark black as mine and thick curly hair cut short on the sides but very tall in the middle, like a mushroom. He peered up at us through round, gold-rimmed glasses.

Danny did some secret handshake with him. "Ladies, may I introduce M.J.—AKA Michael Jordan."

"Michael Jordan?" I asked. "You mean, like the basketball player?"

M.J. slumped. "Yes."

"He hates his name because he can't play basketball," Danny said.

"*At all*," M.J. said.

Danny took a seat beside him. "*And* he's the shortest kid in fifth grade."

Fifth grade! And I'd thought he might be a third grader!

"Second-shortest," M.J. said.

"People in wheelchairs don't count in height competitions," Danny told him.

M.J. looked lasers at him. "Man, do you want my help or not?"

"Yes! Yes," Danny said. He flicked his hair back and motioned for us to sit. "What I didn't tell you about M.J. is that he's like the best computer artist in the whole school."

M.J. looked more pleased to hear that.

"Show 'em what you got, M.J.," Danny said.

M.J. called up a file on the computer. It was a cover of *The Lightning Thief* I'd never seen before, with Percy facing off against the massive minotaur he fights the first time he goes to Camp Half-Blood. It was a great cover.

"What is this?" I asked. "A foreign edition?"

"No, man. This is the M.J. edition."

"You drew this?" Rebecca said.

"On the computer. But yeah," M.J. said.

"Didn't I tell you he was the best?" Danny said.

"How does this help?" Rebecca asked.

"We get M.J. to make up fake covers, and we put them on the books!" I said.

Danny flicked his hair out of his eyes. "Got it in one. See, now anybody drops a book in the cafeteria, Principal Banazewski picks it up, she sees some other book!"

"You'll do it?" I asked. "You'll make us up fake covers for all of our books?"

"Yeah," M.J. said. "But it won't work to have the same cover for all of them. How many books we talking about?"

"Twenty-seven," I told him.

"And more coming," Rebecca said. "We hope."

M.J. whistled. "I better get started. But I'm going to need some titles."

"Real ones?" Danny asked.

"We better not," I said. "If I realized this wasn't a real cover for *The Lightning Thief,* a teacher might too. We need some fake titles."

M.J. opened a word processing document. "I'm all ears."

"Right now?" Rebecca said.

"You want covers, I need titles," M.J. said.

How do you come up with a book title? How do authors come up with book titles? I'd never even thought about it. Book titles always had something to do with what was inside. So how could we come up with book titles for books that weren't real?

Danny combed his hair away from his eyes with his fingers again, and I smiled.

"*The Boy Who Fell in Love with His Hair,*" I said.

M.J. cackled, and started typing.

"Hey! That's not funny," Danny said. He flicked his

hair, then realized what he was doing and blushed. "Here's one for you: *Hair Sucker.*"

I shrank. I didn't know anybody ever noticed me chewing on my braids!

"*Naturally Curly,*" Rebecca said, pretending to primp her black curly hair.

M.J. laughed. "All right, all right. They can't all be about hair."

"We can't say 'sucker' either, or they'll ban that too," Rebecca said.

"*The Girl Who Only Loved Books,*" Danny said.

M.J. nodded. "I like that. I like that. Keep 'em coming."

"*Jessica Rogers, Girl Lawyer,*" Rebecca said.

I shook my head. "Too close to something else."

Rebecca brightened. "Really? What?"

I shook my head again to let her know she really didn't want to read it.

"*The Mystery of the Blue Parrot,*" I said.

"*The Seventeenth Princess,*" Rebecca said.

"*Wet Dog Smell.*"

"*Mr. Bear Opens a Bank Account.*"

"*I Think I Can See My House from Here.*"

"*They Were Already Dead.*"

"*Smell My Finger.*"

"*Tales of a Fourth Grade Zombie.*"

"*Robot Super Ninja!* No. *Super Robot Ninja.* No—*Super Ninja Robot Man.*"

"Danny, it doesn't matter! It's not a real book!"

"I want it to sound good!"

We went back and forth, laughing as we came up with titles, with M.J. typing all the time. We were having so much fun, Mr. Deacon had to tell us to hold it down. I popped up from behind the computer to signal to him we would be quiet, and saw someone in the next row of computers staring right back at me.

Trey McBride.

He waved at me with one hand. His other hand was on the lid of a scanner. The light inside glided back and forth, and he opened it, took his sketch book out, and flipped it over to scan the other side.

I dropped back behind the row of computers, where the other three were swallowing their laughter so hard they were crying.

"Guys," I whispered. "We have to hold it down."

Rebecca nodded, tears rolling down her face. Danny let out something like a honk.

"I'm serious!" I hissed. "Trey's in the next row over! He probably heard everything we said."

That got Rebecca's and Danny's attention. They stopped laughing and peeked over the top of the row.

"Who's Trey?" M.J. asked.

"The son of the lady who banned all these books,"

I told him. But was that all he was? Her son? Or was he her spy too?

"All right. I still need more titles," M.J. said.

"I've got one," I said. "How about, *Friend or Foe?*"

Tra-la-la!

I bounced over to the door where Rebecca and Danny were already in line. Today was the day of Dav Pilkey's author visit! I didn't really like his books, but I'd never met a real live author before. I also had a book of his that I'd just bought for the B.B.L.L. tucked away under my shirt. I wanted to get it autographed. Mr. Vaughn led us to the cafeteria, where we sat in a big half-circle with the rest of the fourth grade. Mrs. Jones stood in the middle of the circle at the projector cart with a man I guessed was Mr. Pilkey. He was white, medium-sized, and not too old, with short brown hair and a flowery Hawaiian shirt. He smiled at something Mrs. Jones said to him, and then she called for our attention.

"All right, fourth graders. I'm very pleased to introduce an author whose books many of you have read and enjoyed. I know I have. Dav Pilkey"—Mrs. Jones said his name like "Dave," even though it was spelled "Dav"—"is the author of more than fifty books, most of which he also illustrated, including *The Dumb Bunnies, Ricky Ricotta,* and of course Captain Underpants. He's also the winner of a Caldecott Honor for *The Paperboy,* and a number of reader's choice awards around the country."

That last part Mrs. Jones said after Principal Banazewski came in the room to stand by the door, I noticed.

"I'm sure Mr. Pilkey will tell you lots more about his life and his books, so I'll turn things over to him. Let's give a big Shelbourne Elementary welcome to Mr. Dav Pilkey!" she said.

Everybody cheered, mostly just for the sake of being able to clap and yell at school, but I cheered because I was really happy he was here.

Mr. Pilkey showed slides of things he had drawn when he was a kid, and told us how he was always getting in trouble at school and getting sent out into the hall to sit by himself. I glanced over at Principal Banazewski when he said that, and she didn't look too happy. The kids around me were all loving it though. Mr. Pilkey was funny, and everybody was laughing. Then Mr. Pilkey talked about when he drew his first comics, and how they weren't spelled right, and didn't look as good as he can draw now, and how none of that mattered because they were a lot of fun and made his friends laugh. You don't have to spell well or be great at grammar to be a writer, he told us, and you don't have to be able to draw perfectly to be an artist. Then he gave examples of famous artists who broke the rules and painted houses upside down, and famous writers who didn't use the right spelling or grammar. Some of the teachers didn't like that so much either.

It wasn't until Mr. Pilkey was in college that a teacher saw his drawings and told him he should be writing and drawing books for kids. That was how he became a kids' book author. He finished his talk, showed us how to draw a picture of Captain Underpants, and asked us if we had any questions. I put my hand up, but so did a lot of other kids. The questions they asked were dumb.

"Did you write all those books?"

"How much money do you make?"

"Where do you get your ideas?"

"I like to draw comics too!" (Which wasn't even a question.)

"Do you know any famous authors?"

"Can you draw Batman?"

And then he called on me.

My heart was racing as I asked, "What do you think about your books being banned from our library?"

The room got very quiet, and I tried very hard not to look at Principal Banazewski.

Mr. Pilkey smiled. "Well, I wish they were on the shelves, where everybody could read them," he said. "I think it's important that libraries be a place where you can find all kinds of books. Good ones, bad ones, funny ones, serious ones. Every person should be free to read whatever they want, whenever they want, and not have to explain to anyone else why we like it, or why we think it's valuable. I hope you all get a chance to read my books someday."

I smiled, my heart still thumping so loud in my chest I thought everyone could hear it. The one copy of Captain Underpants I'd bought before the author visit was going to be checked out forever! I looked over at Principal Banazewski again. She had her arms folded, and was glaring. But not at Mr. Pilkey, and not at me. She was glaring at Mrs. Jones.

People asked more questions (mostly dumb ones), and then Mrs. Jones said we were out of time. Everybody cheered again to thank Mr. Pilkey for being here, and the teachers started dismissing us by class.

"Mr. Vaughn! Mr. Vaughn, can I go and meet the author?" I begged.

He nodded. "Come right back to class afterward," he told me. I grabbed Rebecca and Danny without asking if they could come too and hurried across the room to where Mrs. Jones stood with Mr. Pilkey. Mrs. Jones hugged me while we waited for a couple of kids from another class to be done showing their comics to Mr. Pilkey.

"My little rebel," Mrs. Jones said to me.

Rebel? Me?

The two boys who had drawn the comics were finally called away by their teacher, and we got to say hello.

That's when I realized I couldn't say anything to him about the B.B.L.L. Not with Mrs. Jones standing there. And that's all I'd come to talk about.

Rebecca, Danny, and I just stood there smiling up at him. For a long time. He smiled back like he was waiting for us to say something, but after a while his smile began to falter.

"So . . . do any of you guys like to draw?" Mr. Pilkey asked us.

We all shook our heads.

"Oh. Do you like to write?"

We all shook our heads.

Mr. Pilkey laughed. "Well, you like to read at least, I hope."

"Oh yeah," Rebecca said. "You have no idea."

A student tripped over the cord to the projector cart, and Mrs. Jones hurried away to take care of it. Finally! I looked around once to make sure no one else was watching, and pulled the Captain Underpants book out from under my shirt.

"Will you sign this?" I asked Mr. Pilkey.

He looked surprised, and took the book from me. He looked even more surprised when he saw the cover. "'*Smell My Finger*'?" he said. The cover had a picture of a kid with a stinky finger, and another kid passed out on the ground beside him.

"That's just what's on the outside," I told Mr. Pilkey,

and I opened to the book to show him what was inside: *The Adventures of Captain Underpants.*

"Ohhh," he said. He flipped through it, and found the envelope I'd pasted in the back with the checkout card in it. "*Oh,*" he said. He looked again at the fake cover. "Who did the art?"

"Our friend M.J. He's in fifth grade," Danny said.

"Tell him I said it's great. I should write a real book called *Smell My Finger.*" He looked around to see if anybody was looking. "So I'm guessing your teachers don't know you have this?"

We shook our heads.

"I see." He took a Sharpie from his pocket and opened the book to a front page. "Anybody in particular I should make it out to?"

"The B.B.L.L.," Danny said.

"B.B.L.L.?" he asked. He wrote it in the book—"To the B.B.L.L."—and drew a quick sketch of Captain Underpants saying, "Tra-la-la!" under his signature. "Do I want to know what B.B.L.L. stands for?" he asked as he handed it back.

I stuffed the book up under my shirt. "Probably not," I said.

"All right. Well, keep reading, you guys. And don't get into too much trouble."

Mrs. Jones came back. "Mr. Pilkey, when you're done with these three, I have one more student for you to meet."

I almost squeaked. Mrs. Jones had brought Trey McBride to see the author! Why!? I sucked in my stomach, praying he couldn't see the book under my shirt.

"We have to get back to class!" I said. I grabbed Rebecca and Danny and ran off so fast Mr. Pilkey barely had time to call out "Bye!" to us.

A Present

The Adventures of Captain Underpants never made it to the Banned Books Locker Library. It was checked out before I even got back to class. And it stayed checked out. With a waiting list. I was going to have to save up and buy the rest of them now. I might even have to read it myself.

That afternoon, from my spot in the corner of the library, I watched as Mrs. Jones thanked Mr. Pilkey and helped him get ready to go. He told her he'd had a great time, and thanked her for fighting the good fight. He spotted me watching from the corner, and I ducked back behind *The London Eye Mystery*. When I peeked out again, he had pulled something out of his bag and was whispering something to Mrs. Jones. She looked back at me with a curious expression on her face. Mr. Pilkey's ride to the airport arrived, and he and Mrs. Jones shook hands and said good-bye.

When he was gone, Mrs. Jones called me up to the front desk.

"Mr. Pilkey was very impressed with you, Amy Anne," Mrs. Jones told me. She had that same curious expression on her face, like she was trying to figure something out. "In fact, he left you a present."

A present?

Mrs. Jones looked around the same way I had in the cafeteria to make sure no one was watching, and then brought a boxed set of books up from beneath her desk.

It was every single Captain Underpants book there was. Twelve books.

"For me?" I said.

Mrs. Jones watched me closely. "He said you'd know what to do with them."

I didn't know whether to laugh or cry. This was the biggest single donation in the history of the Banned Books Locker Library!

"I do," I said, and I scooped them up.

"Amy Anne," Mrs. Jones said. "You know not to show these around at school, right?"

I nodded, already thinking about how to get in touch with M.J. as soon as possible.

We were going to need a lot more fake covers.

The Eyes Have It

The very next day, Mrs. Spencer and her friends went through the stacks, looking at every single book.

Mrs. Jones stood a few feet from them, watching them with her arms crossed on her big, blue, polka-dotted dress as they flipped through books looking for anything they didn't like. But there was nothing she could do. Behind them on a table was a tower of books removed for "further review."

I guess Mrs. Spencer didn't like Mrs. Jones's author visit stunt very much.

That afternoon, I called an emergency meeting of the B.B.L.L. board during language arts. Rebecca and Danny and I got library passes and sat at one of the study tables. All around us, the shelves had big holes in them where Mrs. Spencer and her friends had taken books away.

"We have to do something," I told them.

"What?" Rebecca said.

"We have to get copies of all the books they're taking off the shelves," Danny said.

"Where would we put all of them? This is way more than would fit in Amy Anne's locker," Rebecca said.

"My locker," Danny said. "Your locker. We can find room."

"But we don't have enough money to buy them all, and we never will," Rebecca said. "Not even if we had a bake sale every day. Unless Amy Anne can get every author to donate copies like Dav Pilkey."

I sucked on a braid, thinking. "There has to be another way," I said.

"What about it?" Rebecca asked Danny. "You're head of acquisitions."

Danny combed his hair with his fingers. "Well, I actually do have an idea. I know where we can get a copy of every single book taken off the shelves. For free, even."

"Where?"

Danny nodded at the big glass windows that separated Mrs. Jones's office from the rest of the library. I frowned until I saw what he was talking about—the shelf in the back corner of the office where Mrs. Jones kept all the books she'd pulled off the shelves.

Rebecca gasped. "You mean, *steal* them?"

"It's not stealing," Danny said. "They're library books. The whole reason they're here in the first place is to loan out to kids. So we're just borrowing them, right?"

I felt slightly sick at the thought of sneaking into Mrs. Jones's office and taking something, even if it *would* mean we had every book Mrs. Spencer banned.

Danny could see we weren't convinced. "Look, Mrs. Jones bought those books so any kid could read them. That's what we're going to do with them—let any kid read them. She would *want* us to!"

"So why don't we just ask her for them?" Rebecca said.

"Because she can't give them to us," I said. "Not without losing her job. The school board told her not to, and she has to do what the school board says." I stared at the books.

"We can't take all of them, or Mrs. Jones'd notice," Danny said.

"We don't need all of them," I said. "We already have half of them."

"I can't believe we're even considering this!" Rebecca said. "Forget suing us. Theft is a misdemeanor!"

"Does that mean we could go to jail?" I asked.

"Well, no. Not for stealing a few books. Restitution and community service, maybe."

"What's restitution?" Danny asked.

"We have to return the books or pay for them," Rebecca explained. "*And,* it would very likely go down on our permanent record. Which could mean we don't get in to college."

Danny flicked his hair back. "I'm okay with all that."

"Danny!" Rebecca said.

I chewed on my braid. Stealing was bad. I knew that. I hadn't stolen a thing since that lollipop when I was little.

But banning books was worse.

"I make a motion to borrow the books we don't already have in the B.B.L.L. from Mrs. Jones's office," I said.

"Second!" Danny said.

"All those in favor?" I asked.

"Eye!" Danny said, pulling an eyelid down with a finger.

I looked at Rebecca.

"You don't need my yes," she said. "You've already got enough votes."

"You don't have to help if you don't want to," I told her.

Rebecca sighed. "Well, if we get in trouble, I do know a good lawyer. Aye."

"The eyes have it!" Danny said, standing. "Let's do this."

"What, *now?*" Rebecca said.

"Sure," he said. "What are we waiting for? Helen to come?"

"Wait wait wait," I said. "First of all, Mrs. Jones is at the front desk."

"So we'll distract her," Danny said.

"And," I said, "there's an alarm that goes off if you try to take a book out without checking it out, remember?"

"Oh," Danny said. "How do we get around that? Chuck 'em over it?"

I doubted that would work. And I could just see myself trying to catch books out in the hall as Danny tossed them over the scanners. If it was anything like trying to catch a football in gym class, there would be busted books all over the floor. The only way we were going to be able to get away with it was to run the books over that machine at the front desk that demagnetized them, or whatever it did. For some weird reason, that made me think of the picture Trey had drawn for the right to assemble, with the person holding a sign up that said, MAGNETS: HOW DO THEY WORK?

"We'll use the thing on the desk," I told them. "The thing Mrs. Jones runs books over so the alarm doesn't go off. But that means we need a long distraction."

"I got this," Danny said. He pulled a book off one of the shelves around us, opened his messy backpack, and buried it as far down inside as he could.

"What are you going to do?" Rebecca said.

He hefted his backpack onto his shoulder and headed for the door. "I'm going to set off the alarm!"

Rebecca and I hurried around the aisle to where we could watch the entrance and the front desk. My heart was in my throat. I couldn't believe I was about to do this. What kind of person had I become that I would ask an author during a school visit what he thought about his books being banned? Who would steal books from the library to loan them out of my own secret locker library?

Danny stepped between the two white plastic pedestals at the door and the alarm went off. *Wonk-wonk! Wonk-wonk!* Even though it wasn't very loud, the sound of it and the flashing red lights made me and Rebecca both jump. Danny jumped too, even though he'd been expecting it.

Mrs. Jones stirred from her seat at the front desk. "Danny? Do you have a book in your backpack you haven't checked out?"

Danny flicked his hair out of his eyes. "Geez, I don't think so, Mrs. Jones," he said. He tried to go back through, but the alarm went off again.

Mrs. Jones came out from behind her desk and went to him. "Here, let's take a look."

Danny's eyes flicked to mine. It was now or never. I motioned for Rebecca to wait for me and hurried behind Mrs. Jones's desk. I was the one who knew what books we needed, and she could holler if Mrs. Jones was coming back.

I ran to the shelf at the back, my whole body shaking. I skimmed the titles on the spines once all the way through before realizing that I hadn't really read a single word. I was freaking out. I needed to calm down. Think. Reread the titles.

I frowned. Not all of these were on the banned books

list. Then I saw the label on the shelf: REMOVE/RE-PLACE. Some of the books were just old and worn out, and Mrs. Jones was going to order new copies. That would help disguise the fact that I'd taken a few.

I glanced over my shoulder. Rebecca glanced at Danny, who I couldn't see, and back to me. Her eyes told me to hurry, but not to run.

Are You There God? It's Me, Margaret. Matilda. Luv Ya Bunches. The Midwife's Apprentice. Harriet the Spy. The Great Brain. More Adventures of the Great Brain. And Tango Makes Three. The Diary of a Young Girl. The Giver. In the Night Kitchen. Coraline. The Golden Compass. The Face on the Milk Carton. A Day No Pigs Would Die. I went through the list in my head, ticking off all the books that didn't already have little green marks on the sheet hidden behind the GO EAGLES! #1! sign on my locker. When I was finished, I had a stack that reached up to my chin.

I hurried back out to the front desk with them. I was shaking so bad I was sure I was going to trip and spill all the books. I made it to the front desk just as the books were tipping over, but Rebecca helped me catch them. I glanced over at the entrance. Danny was there on the floor, pulling things out of his backpack one at a time for Mrs. Jones.

"There's that language arts assignment!" he said. "I meant to turn that in. And hey! I've been looking for this hairbrush forever!"

"*Hurry,*" Rebecca whispered.

I took the first book to the demagnetizer thing. I didn't really know how the thing worked. Did you have to push a button or something? I didn't see any buttons on it. Instead I just did what Mrs. Jones always does. I stuck the spine of the book into the corner of it and moved it around.

The machine made a little sound—*bonk*—and a light lit up green. Success! I let out a big breath I hadn't realized I'd even been holding. I shoved the book at Rebecca, glanced over at Danny. He pulled a plastic food container out of his backpack. "Oh man, what's growing in that?" he said.

I hurried and rubbed more books over the machine.

"My backpack's full!" Rebecca said when I'd gotten about halfway through.

"Go, go," I told her, and she jog-walked toward the door.

I took a second to watch her go, half afraid Mrs. Jones would somehow psychically know she had the banned books in her bag, and half afraid I hadn't demagnetized them the right way. Rebecca probably had the exact same fears, because she slowed down when she got to Danny and Mrs. Jones. Mrs. Jones had lost her patience with Danny and was looking in his backpack for him. Rebecca shot me a last look, and skipped through the alarms.

It didn't go off! Rebecca was out!

"Here we are," Mrs. Jones said, pulling a book from

Danny's backpack. "*Big Wig: A Little History of Hair,*" Mrs. Jones read.

"*What?*" Danny said. He flicked his hair out of his eyes so he could read it. "Oh. Yeah. It's, um, for a project I'm doing. About hair."

"Well, you'll need to check it out if you want to take it from the library," Mrs. Jones said. Danny looked my way in panic. I still had a small stack of books to demagnetize!

I took a handful of them and stuck them in the machine all at once. The light lit up green. I took the other handful of them and did the same thing. Green. I would just have to hope it took care of all of them. I piled the books in my arms and scurried out from behind the desk just as Mrs. Jones and Danny came over. She hadn't seen me! Now to just stuff these in my backpack, and . . .

But my backpack was already full. It was filled to the top with all the textbooks that wouldn't fit in my locker! What was I going to do?

I looked at the clock. I had to get back to class. Danny was already gone from the front desk. With no other choice, I slipped on my backpack, turned the books around so the titles all faced me, and headed for the exit. Just a few more steps—and then I remembered that I had demagnetized the books in handfuls. Where they all clean, or would one of them give me away?

I held my breath again and stepped between the sensors. Nothing! I was free!

"Amy Anne?" Mrs. Jones called.

I froze. She knew I'd heard her. I couldn't pretend I couldn't.

I turned.

"No good-bye?" Mrs. Jones said with a smile.

I let out a sound that was something between "Oh!" and a frog croaking, then managed a wimpy little "Good-bye" before hurrying away.

The Golden Hoard

I sat on my bed surrounded by books.

I stacked them by size, then stacked them alphabetically, then stacked them by books I'd read and books I hadn't read. I loved the weight of them, the feel of them, especially the hardback books with the clear plastic coating that crinkled and crackled as you opened the book. Some of them were old—older even than I was. Some of them were brand new.

And all of them had been banned.

It was a treasure trove, these stacks, and suddenly I had the idea that I was Smaug the dragon sitting on my piles of gold and jewels, and I would do anything to keep that hobbit and those dwarves from taking them back.

How had I not seen books as treasure before? I loved books. I couldn't imagine living without them. But I had never seen each book as such a valuable thing before. Even the books I wasn't interested in reading were like gold. It didn't matter what was inside them. One man's junk was another man's treasure, as my grandmother said. The same thing was true with books. One person's Captain Underpants was another person's *From the Mixed-up Files of Mrs. Basil E. Frankweiler.*

I didn't have time to sit around thinking about it for too long though. The house was quiet—beautifully, unbelievably quiet—but it wouldn't last. Mom was in the kitchen on her laptop. Angelina was at Gymboree running around like a racehorse, and Alexis was at ballet. In an hour Dad would bring them home, and it would be chaos again. Even the dogs were quiet, curled up and sacked out on Alexis's bed. For the next few minutes my world was all mine, and I had work to do. Work I didn't want anyone else to see me doing.

Some of the books were new enough that they needed card slots pasted into the back. Some of them already had envelopes, and all I had to do was take out the old Shelbourne Elementary library due date card and replace it with one of mine. The old cards were fun to look at. I loved the typewriter font at the top, listing the title and author, and the long lists of scribbled signatures with red due dates stamped beside them. Sometimes you'd see the same name over and over again. I imagined what the card for *From the Mixed-up Files of Mrs. Basil E. Frankweiler* would look like if they still checked books out like this today. My name would be in every slot, and onto the back by now. One girl had checked out *Harriet the Spy* three times. I saw her name again on the *Matilda* card. If I had gone to Shelbourne Elementary in 1985, she and I might have been friends.

I pulled the card out of the next book and skimmed down it, looking for a familiar name. And then I saw one.

A very familiar name.

Was it . . . ? No. *Could it . . . ?* No, it couldn't be. But the more I stared at it, the more I thought, *It has to be.*

That card was a keeper.

Princesses One
through Nine

Jeffrey Gonzalez was back from his suspension.

He sat in his seat in our classroom, arms folded, staring at his empty desk. Everybody else stayed clear of him, but I went up to him before class.

"Hey," I said. "I'm sorry you got suspended."

Jeffrey shrugged. "Whatever."

"I just—I didn't know if you did it for us, or—"

Jeffrey frowned. "What?"

"You know." I lowered my voice. "Because Coletrane dropped that book in the cafeteria. Principal Banazewski was about to pick it up when—"

"I didn't do it for you," Jeffrey said bitterly. "I didn't do it for anybody. He was in my *seat*."

"Okay," I said. "Well, anyway, thanks. Um, live long and prosper."

Live long and prosper was a thing Jeffrey liked to tell people. It was from Star Wars or something.

"Yeah," he said. "Right."

I left Jeffrey under his little black cloud. What was wrong with him? Usually he was drawing spaceships all over his notebook or using the force to try and make the papier-mâché planets that hung from the ceiling spin backward. Now he was just angry all the time.

"All right, everybody. Language arts time," Mr. Vaughn said. "It's Free Reading Friday, so get out whatever you brought to read. I'm going to do the same."

Free Reading Friday was my all-time favorite thing about Mr. Vaughn's class. Every Friday for language arts, we all got to sit around the room and read anything we wanted to—as long as it wasn't a book for school. Even Mr. Vaughn read. He'd been reading an Agatha Christie mystery called *Murder on the Orient Express*. I pulled out *The Mysterious Benedict Society and the Prisoner's Dilemma* and opened it to my bookmark. I was just starting the part where the Mysterious Benedict Society falls into a trap when I heard Mr. Vaughn ask someone across the room, "*The Seventeenth Princess*? What's that about?"

I looked up with a squeak. Danny and Rebecca were gawking too. *The Seventeenth Princess* was one of our fake covers. Someone was reading one of the B.B.L.L. books in class, and Mr. Vaughn had caught her!

It was Lacey Edwards. Lacey was the tallest girl in fourth grade. She looked up at me in horror. The book wasn't about seventeen princesses, of course. Inside, it was *Are You There God? It's Me, Margaret.*

I gave her a look that said, "Make something up!"

Lacey had to look at the cover again to see what the title was.

"It's about . . . the seventeenth princess," she said.

Mr. Vaughn laughed. "Well, I gathered that. What happened to the first sixteen?"

"Well, the first one . . . fell into a pot of boiling oil," Lacey said.

"Ouch," Mr. Vaughn said.

"The second one . . . ate a poisoned apple."

"Always a classic," said Mr. Vaughn.

"The third one . . . got sat on by a giant."

Some of the kids around Lacey laughed. People were starting to pay attention to her.

"The fourth one . . . turned into a werewolf. The fifth one . . . was eaten by a giant shark. The sixth one . . . choked on her own snot."

"Ewwww!" the class said, half-laughing and half-gagging.

I sucked on a braid. Why in the world did we have to make it *seventeen* princesses?

"The seventh princess got kicked in the face with a soccer ball," Lacey said. She was really getting into it now. "The eighth princess . . . she stuck her tongue in an electrical socket!"

The other kids cheered for that one. Mr. Vaughn looked around at them, amused and concerned at the same time.

"The ninth princess accidentally sat on her crown," Lacey said. "The tenth princess—"

"All right, all right," Mr. Vaughn said. "I'm afraid if we go all the way to seventeen, language arts will be over before anyone's done any reading." He shook his head. "That's a strange book you've got there. But it sounds fun."

Mr. Vaughn left Lacey's desk to go sit in the big chair at the front of the room and read his book, and I breathed a huge sigh of relief. I saw Danny and Rebecca do the same thing. That had been a close one. I guess we should be lucky the cover hadn't been *Smell My Finger*.

I was about to go back to my book when I saw one other person looking across the room at me: Trey McBride. He glanced over at Lacey, then back to me, then disappeared behind an Amulet graphic novel.

New Customers

At lunch, Jeffrey sat by himself. He'd had friends before, other kids who liked talking about the same kinds of movies and shows he did. But no one wanted to sit with him now. Jeffrey seemed to want it that way. He picked fights with anybody who hung out with him too long.

I stared across the room at Space Cadet Jeff, feeling sorry for him. He'd always been a nice guy before. He'd been like this for a while now. Ever since . . .

Ever since that day we both got called to the office. He wasn't angry before that. What had Principal Banazewski been telling him as they came out of her office? Something about how she was sure his grandmother had been a nice person.

Jeffrey's grandmother must have died. Was that why he was so mad? I could understand him being sad, but why was he so angry all the time? Then I remembered the books I'd read where people die. Sometimes the characters refuse to believe it. Sometimes they just got to where they shut down and didn't want to do anything. And sometimes they got really mad.

I had a book like that in my locker, in fact.

After lunch, I wrote a note that said I wanted to talk and left it in Jeffrey's locker mailbox. He met me at my locker after school with the note in his hand.

"What?" he said.

"Hey Jeffrey," I said. I didn't know where to start. "I—I know your grandmother died."

Jeffrey looked away, staring at the lockers. "So?" he said.

"I just wanted you to know that I know what you're going through," I said.

His eyes flashed to mine, and I saw the Jeffrey who'd gotten suspended for fighting. "Oh yeah?" he said. "Did *your* grandmother die?"

"N-no," I said.

"Then you *don't* know," he said.

"But I've read about it," I said. "In a book."

Jeffrey snorted and looked away. I opened my locker and showed him the book.

"*Mr. Bear Opens a Bank Account*?" he said.

"Oh. No. That's just the fake cover we put on it to fool the teachers." I opened it up to show him. "It's called *Bridge to Terabithia*. I think you should read it."

Jeffrey looked at the book in my hands but didn't take it.

"It sounds stupid," Jeffrey said.

"It's not. It's really good," I told him. "It's about these two kids who invent this pretend kingdom and become the king and queen. I think you'll really like it."

I held the book out to Jeffrey, and he finally took it.

"I'll maybe read it," he said.

"Okay," I said. I hoped he would.

Jeffrey walked away and I turned. Trey McBride was standing right behind me. I jumped out of my skin, then remembered to slam my locker shut and slip on the lock.

"Hey," Trey said.

"Hey," I said back. I tried not to sound nervous, even though I was. Every time I turned around, there he was! He stood there for a few seconds, just looking at me but not saying anything. What did he want? Our First Amendment project was already finished.

"I want to borrow a book," Trey said.

What!? I swallowed. Hard. "The school library is right down the hall," I told him.

"I want to borrow a book from you. From your locker."

"I don't know what you're—"

"I want to borrow Captain Underpants," he told me. "I know you have it."

Trey flipped up the GO EAGLES! #1! sign on my locker and pointed to the list of banned books on the back. "The green dots mean you have them, right? I want to read this one."

My own little patch of quicksand was opening up underneath me again. Trey knew all about the B.B.L.L. Did that mean his mom knew too? Maybe she did. Maybe Trey had figured it out, and told his mom, but instead of going right to the principal, she'd sent him here to check out a book. As evidence.

I shook my head. I was beginning to think like Rebecca.

"No, you don't have it? Or no, you won't let me check it out?" Trey asked. He'd taken my head shake for a no.

I didn't know what to tell him. If I gave him the book and he took it to his mom, it was all over, and I was in big trouble. But what if Trey really just wanted to read the book? Didn't all this start when he checked out Captain Underpants from the school library to read it? I'd gotten to know Trey working together on our First Amendment project, and I'd started to like him—despite him drawing me as a mouse in third grade. And it was Trey's mom who banned the books, not Trey. Maybe he didn't agree with her at all.

Maybe he just really wanted to read Captain Underpants.

And that's why I had the Banned Books Locker Library to begin with, wasn't it? So anybody who wanted to could read the books banned from the school library?

Trey looked disappointed in me, and turned to leave.

"Wait," I said. "I do have one. And . . . you can borrow it."

I was saying all kinds of crazy things out loud these days.

I spun the dial on my lock, yanked it open, and got out Captain Underpants.

Trey's eyes lit up. "Do you have the fourth one? *Captain Underpants and the Perilous Plot of Professor Poopypants?*"

I did.

My Biggest Mistake

I knew I was in trouble from the moment I set foot in the building Monday morning.

It was in the way the other kids stared at me, then turned to their friends to whisper. The way everybody moved out of my way, like I was Hagrid parting crowds in Diagon Alley. The way my sneakers squeaked loud enough for me to hear them in the quiet hall.

A chill ran down my spine, and I got goosebumps. And not the R. L. Stine kind. My footsteps slowed and my heart pounded in my chest. Something was wrong here. Very, very wrong.

And then I turned the corner and saw Principal Banazewski standing next to my locker. Mr. Crutchfield, the Shelbourne Elementary custodian, stood next to her with the long-handled metal cutters he used to cut off locks when kids forgot their combinations.

No, I thought. *No, no, no, no, no.*

"Miss Ollinger," Principal Banazewski said. "I need you to open your locker, please."

I started crying. I couldn't help it, even with everybody watching. Tears streamed down my face, and I sobbed once. This couldn't be happening. Mrs. Banazewski wasn't really standing in front of my locker telling me to open it. I was still asleep. I was dreaming. I had to be. This was a nightmare. Because if Mrs. Banazewski was there, telling me to open my locker, that meant it was all over.

"Miss Ollinger, if you won't open the lock, I'll have to ask Mr. Crutchfield to cut it off."

I wanted to say something. I wanted to do something. But all I did was stand there and cry. I was barely even aware of all the other kids who'd gathered around to gawk.

"All right, Mr. Crutchfield," Principal Banazewski said.

Through watery eyes, I watched him slip the cutters around my lock and squeeze. The lock popped, and Mrs. Banazewski removed it.

The hallway was completely silent as Principal Banazewski opened my locker. The *chik-chink* of the handle on my locker echoed in the quiet. It sounded like handcuffs going on my wrists. I wanted to fall to my knees. Where was my quicksand? I wanted it now. I wanted to be swallowed up by the ground and disappear forever, but there I stood, watching through my tears as Principal Banazewski pulled books out of my locker library. The covers didn't fool her for a second. She already knew. She opened one, then another, then another, until she was satisfied they were illegal books.

They all were. My locker was stacked full of them, from top to bottom. I let the backpack filled with my schoolbooks slide to the ground.

"Mr. Crutchfield, if you'll collect all the books in this locker and bring them to my office?" Principal Banazewski said. "Miss Ollinger, you'll come to the office with me, and we'll call your parents."

I followed along, numb. I saw Rebecca, her hand to her mouth and tears running down her face. I saw Danny, whose pained eyes stared out from under his perfect hair. I saw Javy, and Janna, and Parker, and Sophia, and Felisha, and T.J., and a bunch of other people who'd borrowed books from the B.B.L.L. They watched me get taken away like a criminal.

And there, at the end of the hall, was Trey. His mother stood behind him, her hands on his shoulders, looking at me like I had just slapped her in the face.

Loaning that book to Trey had been the biggest mistake of my life.

Busted

My parents were called in. Mom had to get pulled out of a meeting. Dad still had on his work overalls, and his hands were covered in red brick dust. At first they thought I was hurt, or that someone had done something awful to me. They never guessed I was the one who had gotten into trouble. I was Amy Anne Ollinger. I was the girl who always did what her parents and teachers told her to. I was the girl who never complained, never spoke up, never said what she was really thinking.

Principal Banazewski showed them the books. Told my parents what I'd been doing. My parents looked at me like they'd never seen me before.

"Some of these are Shelbourne Elementary library books," Principal Banazewski said. She had them separated out in a stack on her desk, next to the grinning banana in sunglasses. They were all the books we'd taken from Mrs. Jones's office, minus the ones that were checked out. "Did Mrs. Jones give you these books?"

"No!" I said. I didn't want Mrs. Jones to get into trouble over this. Just the thought of that made me even sicker than I was over getting caught.

"Are you saying you stole school property then?" Principal Banazewski said.

I didn't say anything.

"Amy Anne, this is no time to protect anybody," Mom said. "Mrs. Jones is an adult. She's responsible for her own actions."

"She didn't know!" I said. "We took those books from the library. It's not stealing if you borrow a library book. That's what they're for."

"Who is 'we'?" Mrs. Banazewski asked.

Stupid stupid stupid! I hadn't meant to say that.

"Nobody. I did it all by myself," I said.

Principal Banazewski frowned. "You're not going to tell me who else was in on this with you?"

I hesitated, then shook my head and looked at the floor.

"Amy Anne!" Mom said.

I didn't care how much more trouble I was going to get into. I wasn't going to drag Rebecca and Danny down with me.

"We'll find out," Principal Banazewski said. "We'll be able to get back all the books she's loaned out to other students too. We have a list of all the students who checked out books from her little illegal library." She lifted a stack of index cards. My date due cards! I closed my eyes, and the tears came again. I should have listened to Rebecca: never leave a paper trail.

"I'm going to have to write a letter home to the parents of each and every one of these children, Amy Anne, explaining how an inappropriate and potentially harmful book came into their possession at my school," Principal Banazewski said. "There may even be lawsuits. You've hurt a lot of other people with this little stunt."

Principal Banazewski waited for me to say something in my defense, but I was done speaking up. For good.

"As this is Amy Anne's first major offense, she won't be expelled," Principal Banazewski said. "But for theft of school property and for willfully defying the Wake County School Board, Amy Anne is suspended for three days."

Right and Wrong

I couldn't very well stay with my dad at a construction site, so I spent the day in my mom's office. I did the homework Mr. Vaughn had sent me home with, then hid in the corner reading *Indian Captive*, which I'd checked out from the real school library. When I finished it, I just read it again. Like Mary Jemison, I swore I would bear my pain quietly, and without complaint. If I had been quiet before, I was going to be silent from now on. Speaking up just got you into trouble.

Mom didn't have much to say to me all day anyway. I could tell she was still thinking about what to say, and how to punish me. Because getting suspended from school wasn't going to be enough. Parents can't ever let the bad stuff that happens when you make a mistake be all there is to it. They always have to add on some punishment of their own too, to remind you that they're in charge.

That afternoon I went to my room without being told to and crawled under the blankets on my bed. Normally

Alexis would have been using my bed for a ballet barre, but today she kept away. She snuck in once to get her tutu, then slipped out again without saying a word. That was fine with me.

I tried reading *Indian Captive* again, but I couldn't focus on it. All I could think about was all the kids who had borrowed books from me. They were all going to get letters sent home from school, and a lot of them were going to get in trouble. And it was my fault. Everybody who'd started to like me was going to hate me now.

Dad brought me my dinner on a tray and told me I was to come and see him and Mom both in the kitchen when I was done.

No matter how slowly I ate, I knew I couldn't put it off forever. Halfway through I couldn't eat any more anyway. It was time to face my parents.

Dad was doing the dishes when I came in. I sat at the table, and he called Mom in and dried his hands. The air felt heavier in the kitchen, like someone had just died.

Angelina appeared in the doorway. "Is Amy Anne in trouble?" she asked.

"Yes, genius," I thought. But I didn't say it. I was done talking.

"Go back to the living room," Mom said. "Alexis? Come get your sister, and keep her in the living room, please."

There were to be no witnesses to my execution.

When Alexis and Angelina were gone, Mom and Dad shared another of those looks. This one I could read. It said, "We better get this over with." I started to suck on my braids, but I knew that would just make Mom more frustrated, so I fought the temptation.

"Amy Anne, we don't know where to begin," Dad said. "We're just so shocked that you would do this. It's so unlike you."

I didn't say anything.

"We're very disappointed," Mom said. "We expect better out of you. We expect you to set an example for your sisters."

I didn't think I had any more tears left in me, but I started crying again.

"On the other hand," Dad said, "we're proud of you for taking a stand." Mom and Dad shared another of those looks between them. "Frankly, we were getting worried that you *never* stand up for yourself. Never speak up."

I hiccupped a sob. "What good does it do to speak up when no one listens to what I'm saying?" I thought. But I didn't say it.

"Keeping all that inside isn't healthy," Mom said. "And we agree, there are times you have to stand up for what you want."

"Or what's right," Dad said. "We don't necessarily agree with Principal Banazewski and the school board on this book banning business."

I sniffed and rubbed my nose with my hand. I couldn't believe what I was hearing. Was I not going to get more punishment?

"But there's a right way and a wrong way to voice your objections," Mom said, "and this banned book library in your locker was the wrong way."

Right. So I was getting more punishment after all.

"You broke the rules, kiddo," Dad said.

"Right or wrong, the school board made a decision that those books weren't appropriate for elementary school students, and you have to respect that decision," Mom said. "You can't just decide what an adult tells you is wrong and do whatever you want."

But what if the adult was *wrong*? Mom and Dad *just said* they didn't agree with the school board. And what if the adults didn't play by their own rules? What was a kid supposed to do then? Just give up and do whatever they said? I wanted to argue with them, but I didn't. I just sat and stared at the table.

"We'll deal with whatever else comes of this," Dad said. "I think Mrs. Banazewski's threat about lawsuits was a bit much. But I do think there are going to be some pretty angry parents. That little woman who spoke at the school board meeting isn't going to be very happy."

I didn't really care how Mrs. Spencer felt. Or her stupid son, for that matter.

"There's something else we need to talk about, Amy

Anne," Mom said. "Something even more disturbing to us. In talking with Principal Banazewski, we've also discovered that you haven't been attending any of the after-school activities you told us you've been doing."

I reeled. This, on top of the B.B.L.L. suspension? I was totally blindsided.

"Why have you been staying late after school if you're not in any of these clubs?" Dad asked.

"Because I need some time by myself! Because I don't have a quiet place of my own where I can just curl up in the corner with a book and read!" I wanted to tell them.

But I didn't say anything.

"More than anything, I think it's the lying that hurts me most, Amy Anne," my mother said.

I started to cry again. I couldn't look either of them in the face. I felt sick for lying to them.

"Your father and I have decided to ground you for a week," Mom said. "We know that doesn't mean much though, since all you'd do is sit in your room and read books. So we're not allowing you to read anything that isn't for a school assignment either."

I felt dizzy. Not read for an entire week? What was I going to do? How was I going to survive? I was suspended, everyone at school hated me, and I had nowhere to hide. My books were all I had left. My sobs overtook me.

The phone rang, and Dad got up to answer it.

"Hello? Yes . . . Oh. No, I don't think that would be a

good idea . . . No. Thank you, but no." He hung up. "That was the local news," Dad said. He sighed. "The story's out. They were calling to see if they could interview Amy Anne about the locker library."

"Great," Mom said. "That's just what we need. All right, Amy Anne. Go on to your room. Tomorrow you'll have to come in to the office with me again. Bring your schoolbooks. But no other books. Understand?"

I nodded and hurried away.

Alexis wasn't in our room when I got there. I ran inside and threw myself on the bed, burying my face in my pillow to cry. I had ruined everything. *Everything.* My friends were never going to talk to me again. My parents were never going to trust me again. Nobody was ever going to think of me as the good girl who did what she was told ever again.

The dogs hopped up on my bed and stuck their wet noses in my neck, trying to make me feel better.

"Amy Anne?"

It was Angelina. She was standing in the door to my room. The dogs must have come with her. She and Alexis must have been loving this.

"Go away," I told her, my face still buried in my pillow.

The dogs laid down with me and the room got quiet, and I guessed Angelina had gone. Then I felt something nudge my arm, something soft and furry that wasn't one of the dogs. I opened my eyes.

Angelina was gone, but she had left me her favorite stuffed pony to make me feel better.

The Latest Casualty

I was in my room that night planning my escape to the Cameron Village library, *From the Mixed-up Files*–style, when I heard something about Shelbourne Elementary on the television in the living room. It was late—the new glow-in-the-dark alarm clock I'd gotten for my birthday said it was 11:10 P.M.—and Alexis was already asleep across the room. I slipped out of bed and tiptoed down the hall to peek in at the TV. They were showing pictures of my school while a woman explained all about the Banned Books Locker Library. They even showed a picture of me from last year's yearbook! I squeaked, but covered my mouth enough that Mom and Dad didn't hear me. On the couch, I saw my mom put her hand to her forehead, like she had a headache.

Mrs. Spencer came on then. "Fourth graders aren't old enough to make decisions like this for themselves," she said. "That's why they have parents. That's why we have a school board. The school board agreed that these books were inappropriate for elementary school students—in many cases harmful. The books were removed from the library for their protection."

The reporter talked about how this all began, with the school board meeting where Mrs. Spencer got them to remove the books, and then a picture of Mrs. Jones came up on the screen.

"At the center of the controversy is Shelbourne Elementary librarian Dr. Opal Jones, who all along has maintained that the books should remain available to all students."

Mrs. Jones, decked out in a blue dress with white polka dots, appeared in a recorded interview. "Every parent has the right to decide what their child can and can't read. What they cannot do is make that decision for everyone else," she said. It was the same thing she'd said at the school board meeting.

"Tonight, Mrs. Jones became the latest casualty in what observers are calling 'The Battle of the Books,'" the reporter said.

The report cut to a man in a suit. Under his name, it said he was a member of the school board.

"Whether deliberately or through negligence, Dr. Jones let those books circulate, against the express orders of the school board. As such, her contract has been terminated."

Her contract has been terminated. That meant fired.

Mrs. Jones had been fired, and it was all because of me.

My Glorious Return

Dad drove me to school my first day back from suspension so I wouldn't have to ride the bus. I didn't want to have to sit there while Rebecca and Danny pretended to not know me. They probably still liked me, but now I was the girl who got everybody in trouble. They couldn't hang out with me anymore, or everybody would hate them too. I didn't blame them, but I just couldn't bear it. Not on my first day back.

Dad knew I was scared to go back. He didn't even tell me not to suck on my braids. I don't know if he did it on purpose or not, but he dropped me off with a kiss right as the first bell rang, so everyone was already in class when I walked down the hall. I was going to get a tardy slip, but I wasn't too worried about it. Not like I would have been before. I wasn't the good girl anymore. I had just been suspended for three days. Being on time for class didn't really seem all that important anymore.

I was glad nobody was there when I got to my locker.

Every day I went straight to my locker and put in the combination on my lock to open it. But the lock was gone, of course. Mr. Crutchfield had cut it off. Suddenly it was three days ago, and I was standing exactly where I was now and I was watching Principal Banazewski open my locker and pull out all the banned books, and I was crying in front of everyone.

I started to cry again now, but not as bad. Just a tear or two. I wiped my eyes with the back of my hand. I was going to have to open my locker again, put my books in, and get to class. At least now it would be empty, and I could put all my schoolbooks in there without having to lug them around.

But it wasn't empty. When I opened my locker, folded notes spilled out of it onto the floor. Dozens of them. My locker mailbox had been stuffed full, and when more notes wouldn't fit they'd piled up inside my locker. I opened one with pink loopy handwriting.

> *AA—*
> *I'm sorry you got suspended!!!!!!!! Hang in there.*
> *—Janna*

Another one said,

> *Dear Amy Anne,*
> *My parents got a letter telling them I checked*

out a book from the B.B.L.L., but they didn't
care. It stinks that you got suspended. Principal
Banana is a doofus.

—Kevin

They were all like that. Fourth graders writing to tell me they were sorry I got suspended. That Principal Banazewski and the school board were wrong. That their parents had gotten the letter Mrs. Banazewski said she would write, but either their parents didn't care or they didn't care that their parents were upset.

I sat on the floor and opened every one. I cried again as I read them, but this time I wasn't crying because I was sad. I was crying because everybody was being so nice.

I stuffed all the letters into my locker with my books, dried my eyes, and opened the door to Mr. Vaughn's classroom. Mr. Vaughn was in the middle of reading out a new list of vocabulary words when every head in the room turned and saw me. Rebecca squealed, jumped up, and ran across the room to hug me. Danny came over too, but just stood nearby smiling at me. Everybody else broke out cheering and clapping. Everybody but Trey.

I was stunned by my class's response. I was sure everyone was going to hate me.

"I tried to call, but your mom said you were grounded!" Rebecca said.

"Did you see all the notes?" Danny said. "I told everyone the truth about why you got suspended."

I didn't have a chance to answer them. Mr. Vaughn quieted everyone down and sent us to our seats. "All right, all right," he said. "Welcome back, Amy Anne. As you can see, you were missed by everyone, including me. Now, if we can try to focus on our new vocabulary list? The next word is 'valiant.'"

As soon as we got to a time when we could all get up and move around, Rebecca and Danny and a few of the other students hurried over to me. I worried that Mr. Vaughn was going to make us be quiet and separate us, but he pretended to be focused on something at his desk and not notice.

"I saw your picture on the news!" Danny said, flicking his hair out of his face.

"Did you hear? Mrs. Jones was fired!" Rebecca said.

"I know," I said. It still hurt to think about it. "Did you guys get in trouble?"

"Nah," Danny said. "I mean, we got the letter home, like everybody else. But that's it."

"There's going to be a special school board meeting," someone else said. "My mom said I can go!"

"Me too!" some of the others added.

"What are we going to do now?" Danny asked me.

"What do you mean?" I asked.

"What's next?" Rebecca said. "How do we get Mrs. Jones and all the books back?"

Get Mrs. Jones and the books back? How was that even possible? And how on earth did they think I would know the answer? It was over. The B.B.L.L. was finished, and so was I.

But I didn't say that. All I said was, "I—I don't know."

"Well, just wait till Helen comes," Danny said. "Then they'll be sorry."

"We don't have to wait till Helen comes," Rebecca said. "We've got Amy Anne."

Mr. Vaughn coughed, which told us it was time to get back to doing some real work. Rebecca and Danny smiled at me as they left, which made me feel even worse. What was everybody going to think of me when they realized there was nothing I could do—that there was nothing any of us could do—to fix everything?

I looked up and saw Trey watching me from across the room. My fists clenched and my face got hot. In the three days since I'd been suspended, I'd felt sad, then sorry, then hopeless, then depressed. But now I was just mad, and I was starting to think that giving Trey a big old knuckle sandwich might just be worth another three days of suspension.

The Mirror Universe

I was marching across the cafeteria to give Trey a piece of my mind—and maybe a piece of my fist—when Jeffrey Gonzalez appeared in front of me like somebody transporting in one of those science-fiction shows he watched. I almost knocked him over.

"Hey Amy Anne," he said.

"Hey Jeffrey," I said. "Excuse me. I need to go and punch somebody in the face."

Jeffrey looked nervously behind him, wondering who I was talking about. "Oh. Okay," he said. "I just wanted to say I was sorry. You know. For getting you suspended."

I stopped. "What?"

"I'm sorry I got you suspended," Jeffrey said. He looked a little worried I was going to punch him instead.

"How did you get me suspended?" I asked.

"It was that book you gave me. *Bridge to Terabithia*. I

read it, and it . . . it made me think about my Grammy. My grandmother who . . . who died. When I finished it, I just—I got really upset."

My heart sank. I felt awful. I hadn't meant for *Bridge to Terabithia* to make Jeffrey feel bad. I had thought that maybe reading about somebody else who lost someone suddenly would make him understand he wasn't alone. Maybe show him there was a way out of the sadness.

"No, no—not like that," he said, seeing the worry on my face. "I mean, it made me cry." Jeffrey looked around, embarrassed. "And I couldn't stop crying. That's when Mom and Dad came in my room, and I kind of let it all out. I hadn't really cried since Grammy died. I guess I needed to. Anyway, Mom and Dad saw it was the book that did it, so they called the principal. But not because they were mad. They called to say how great it was that Mrs. Jones gave me the book."

I saw it all in my head. Jeffrey's parents call to tell Principal Banazewski how Mrs. Jones helped Jeffrey by giving him the right book. Oh, how wonderful! Mrs. Banazewski says. What book? *Bridge to Terabithia,* they say. Alarm bells go off for Principal Banazewski. She's heard of that book. It was on the banned books list. She goes to Mrs. Jones. Mrs. Jones says she never gave anybody that book. It's right back here on the shelf. Only it isn't. But then where did Jeffrey get it?

"They made me tell!" Jeffrey said. "I'm so sorry! I never meant to get you in trouble, and neither did my parents. They're real sorry too. They said they would call your parents and let them know."

I looked at Trey across the room, drawing in his sketchbook. A minute ago, I was ready to kill him for ratting me out. But it turned out he didn't have anything to do with it after all.

"It's okay," I told Jeffrey. "I'm just glad you feel better. You got really mean there for a little while."

"I know," Jeffrey said. "That was the Mirror Universe me."

"The Mirror Universe you?"

"Yeah," he said. "In *Star Trek,* there's this Mirror Universe, and everybody there is the opposite of what they are in this universe. So if you're good here, you're bad there. The Mirror Universe Jeffrey took over for a little while, but Jeffrey Prime is back now."

He was losing me. "Well, whoever you are now, I'm glad you're back."

Jeffrey smiled and saluted me with his fingers in a V shape. "Live long and prosper," he told me.

"You too," I said.

Instead of marching across to Trey, I went and stood in the cafeteria line, thinking about the Mirror Universe Amy Anne. Which one was the good one, and which one was the bad one? The Amy Anne who never spoke up and never got into trouble, or the Amy Anne who refused to accept a bad decision by the school board and did something good about it?

The Biggest Idea

The library was a very different place without Mrs. Jones in it.

I stood at the entrance between the two pedestals with the book detectors in them, but even from there I could feel the difference. It was quieter in the library. And sadder. It made my chest ache, like when I'd fallen off my bike and gotten the wind knocked out of me. The library had been the only place in the world I loved. The only place that felt like it was all mine, even if other people were there at the same time. The school library had been my home. But this wasn't my home—or my library—anymore.

I didn't want to go one step farther into that place, but I needed to return *Indian Captive*. I crept up to the front desk. There was another lady sitting there. A substitute for Mrs. Jones. She was a big white woman, like Mrs. Jones, and had glasses on a chain, just like Mrs. Jones, only hers were square. She wore a colorful dress like Mrs. Jones too, only it was red-and-white stripes, not polka dots.

She looked up from a copy of one of those celebrity gossip magazines and said, "Yes?"

It was creepy. Mrs. Jones should be sitting there, not this person. Then I realized who she was: *She was the Mirror Mrs. Jones!*

"I'm just returning a book!" I said. I dropped it on the counter and ran.

Right into Trey McBride.

Neither of us fell down, but a stack of papers he'd been carrying went flying all over the floor.

"Sorry! Sorry," I said.

"Shh!" Mirror Mrs. Jones said. The real Mrs. Jones never shushed people in the library.

I immediately bent to help Trey pick up his papers, until I finally saw what it was I was picking up.

"Wait. What is this?" I asked him.

"It's—"

"They're Request for Reconsideration forms." The forms Mrs. Jones was always telling Trey's mom she had to fill out if she wanted to challenge a book. I flipped through them. Each and every one was a Request for Reconsideration form for a different book that hadn't been banned. Not yet. These forms were asking that they all be removed from the library. But that wasn't the worst part. The worst part was that they hadn't been filled out by Mrs. Spencer.

"These are all in your handwriting!" I said.

"No talking!" Mirror Mrs. Jones barked, making me jump.

I pushed the papers back into Trey's hands and kept on pushing him back out into the hall.

"You're as bad as your mom!" I yelled at him when we were out of the library.

"I—" he started to say.

"It's bad enough that she already banned half the books in the library. Now you have to go and ban the other half?" I said. I didn't know if this was the real Amy Anne or the Mirror Amy Anne, but she was back, and she wasn't going to be quiet anymore.

"You—" Trey tried to say, but I cut him off.

"At first I hated you," I told him. "You drew that awful picture of me as a mouse last year and hurt my feelings. Then we had to work together on our Bill of Rights project and I thought you were different and I started to like you. Then I thought you ratted me out and got the Locker Library busted, and I hated you all over again."

Trey frowned. "But—"

"Then I found out it *wasn't* you who turned me in, and I started to like you again. And now this!" I snatched some of the papers back from him and read out titles he wanted to ban. "*Sounder*? *The Indian in the Cupboard*? The Chronicles of Prydain? *My Teacher Is an Alien*? *The Kid Who Only Hit Homers*? Are you kidding with this?"

"If you'd just let me—"

"What's going to happen when you challenge every single book in this library?" I asked him. "What then, Trey? I'll tell you what will happen. You challenge every book in the library for every stupid little reason you can think of, and there won't be a single book left on the shelves for anyone to check out!"

"*Exactly*," Trey said.

"You—what?" I said. I didn't understand. That was seriously what he was trying to do?

"Are you finished?" Trey said. "Can I talk now?"

I nodded, still confused.

"Okay, first, you hated me because of the picture I drew of you last year?"

My face burned hot. I couldn't believe I'd actually told him that. But this was the new Amy Anne. The one who wasn't going to keep quiet anymore. I took a deep breath. "Yes," I said. "You drew me as a mouse!"

"Reading a book," Trey said.

"But I'm a mouse! Everybody else was lions and eagles and cheetahs and things! Mice are—"

"Quiet?" Trey said. "Timid?"

I huffed. "Yes."

"So were you. I mean, you're not *now*," he said, straightening his shirt from where I'd pushed him. "But you always had your nose in a book and never said anything. And whenever anybody *did* say something to you, it was like you were having this conversation with them in your head but you never said any of it out loud."

"That's crazy," I wanted to tell him. "I don't have conversations with other people in my head!" Then I blushed. He was right. I did it all the time. I was doing it again right now!

"You're right," I said. I hated to admit it, but it was true.

"I'm sorry it hurt your feelings," Trey said. "I didn't mean it to. It's just how I saw you. I wouldn't draw you the same way now."

"Okay, so what's the deal with these Request for Reconsideration forms?" I asked him.

Trey smiled. "What better way to show everybody how stupid it is to ban books than to take it as far as it can go? Once you ban one book, you can ban them all." He tried to straighten the mess of papers in his arms. "This is just a start. When I'm finished, there won't be one book left on the Shelbourne library shelves. Just wait until the TV cameras get a load of that!"

"So . . . you don't really want these books banned?" I asked.

"I never wanted *any* books banned," Trey said. "That was all my mom's idea. I like Captain Underpants. I'm trying to draw a book just like it."

Of course. Trey's mom hadn't known about Captain

Underpants until he'd checked it out from the library in the first place. And every time I saw him, Trey was drawing. That must have been why Mrs. Jones introduced him to Dav Pilkey! She knew he was trying to draw a book like Captain Underpants.

"I'm sorry," I told him. "I always thought you agreed with your mom."

"So did everybody else," Trey said.

I nodded to the forms in his hands. "If you do this, if you get all these books banned, everybody's going to think you really do agree with her."

Trey shrugged. "It doesn't matter now. Everybody already hates me because of her."

I felt awful. I'd done the same thing—blamed him for what his mom was doing.

"I'm the one to do it," Trey said. "Maybe in the end everybody'll see why I did it. If they don't kill me first."

"There's thousands of books," I said. "It'll take you all year. And they'll probably figure out what you're trying to do before you can finish."

Trey shrugged again. "I have to do something."

I knew exactly what he meant. It was the same way I felt when I started the B.B.L.L. And it was exactly the same way I felt now.

"Don't turn those in," I told him. "Not yet. Turn them all in at once."

"When?" he said. "Like you said, that'll take forever. It needs to happen now. While people still care."

"I know," I said. "Which is why we're going to need some help."

"*We?*" said Trey.

"We," I said.

Twenty-four Farts

Mr. Vaughn's class was in the library. We were supposed to be looking for new books to read, but the B.B.L.L. board had other plans. Rebecca, Danny, and I met back in the stacks, as far away from the Mirror Mrs. Jones as we could get. The first order of business was to add Trey McBride as our newest member.

"*Trey?*" Danny asked.

Trey was there, and he looked embarrassed.

"He wasn't the one banning books. It was his mom," I said. "And you know how you were asking me what we do next? He's got a plan. I move that we add him to the B.B.L.L. board as . . . our challenge response coordinator."

That got Rebecca and Danny interested. He was voted in unanimously.

"So here's what we're going to do," I told them. "We're going to ban every book in this library."

Rebecca and Danny looked as stunned as I had been.

"Ban every book?" Rebecca said.

"Shh!" called Mirror Mrs. Jones. "No talking!"

I dragged the B.B.L.L. board into one of the library meeting rooms where we could talk, and explained the plan. When Rebecca and Danny got it, they liked it. I knew they would.

Danny flicked his hair out of his eyes. "But how are we going to find something wrong with every book?"

"Trust me," Trey said, "books have been challenged for all kinds of crazy reasons. I looked up some challenges on the Internet. The easy ones are anything that's got witch-craft or supernatural stuff in it, anything with bad words, anything with gay characters, anything with violence, and anything that mentions sex in it." He blushed when he said the last one, and we all found somewhere else to be looking.

"That's a lot of books," Rebecca said, "but not nearly all of them."

"But look at this." Trey unfolded a piece of paper on the table. "*The Stupids* got challenged because it 'reinforces negative behavior' and 'might encourage children to dis-obey their parents.' Here's a riddle book that got banned because it made kids who couldn't figure out the riddles feel bad. *My Teacher Is an Alien* got challenged because it 'portrays the main character as handling a problem on her own, rather than relying on the help of others.' Here's 'de-struction of property,' 'teaches kids to lie,' 'a real downer,' 'anti-family,' 'lewd,' 'twisted,' 'too mature,' 'too immature,' 'bad grammar,' *promotes poor nutrition,* 'includes the word fart twenty-four times—'"

Danny snorted. "What book is *that*?"

"*Walter the Farting Dog.*"

"Oh, sure," Danny said, and we all nodded.

"Look, the point is, once you ban one book, somebody, somewhere, can find a reason to ban *every* book," I said. I looked to Trey, and he nodded.

"Even *Where's Waldo?* has been banned because somebody found one little woman sunbathing facedown with her top off," Trey said. "We just have to start thinking like people who see stuff everywhere that bothers them."

"So . . . I just have to pretend to be my grandmother," Rebecca said.

"Or my mom," said Trey.

A Lawsuit
Waiting to Happen

Once we got into looking for reasons to ban books, it was kind of fun.

Anything with witches, wizards, jack-o'-lanterns, demons, or gods: gone. No Harry Potter, no Percy Jackson, no Artemis Fowl, no Chronicles of Narnia.

Anything about sex or the human body or reproduction: gone.

Anything with gay characters in it: gone.

"This one says 'Oh lord' in it," Danny said. "My mother won't let me say God's name unless I'm praying."

"Ban it," I told him.

"This book has the word 'scrotum' on the first page!" Trey said.

I looked at the cover. It was a Newbery winner. "Yeah, just about anything with one of these medals on it, you can find some reason to ban it. Fill out a form," I told him.

"Shh! No talking!" Mirror Mrs. Jones yelled.

We worked quietly and quickly all week long. That book about the Civil War? Too violent. That book about the Holocaust? Too depressing. That book about diseases? Too scary. A book about lions? Too gory. Every night, I took home a stack of Request for Reconsideration forms to add to the growing pile in my bedroom. We were going to bring them all to the next school board meeting. Really put on a show when all the TV cameras would be there. But we only had four school days left, and lots more books to ban.

Luckily we had Rebecca. She was the one who really shone when it came to challenging books. If ever there was a book we just couldn't imagine anybody banning, Rebecca could always come up with a reason. I think it was all the time she'd spent practicing to be a lawyer.

"*The Lorax*? That's libelous. *The Lorax* portrays lumberjacks and the timber industry in a negative light.

"*Goodnight Moon*? The mouse in the room is a healthcode violation, the red balloon is a choking hazard, and look at this picture of the illustrator on the back—he's holding a cigarette! That encourages kindergarteners to think smoking is cool.

"Oh, and don't get me started about *Amelia Bedelia*. She clearly has Asperger's syndrome, and yet children are encouraged to laugh at her? What kind of message is that sending?

"This library is a lawsuit waiting to happen!" Rebecca told me. There was a gleam in her eye as she said it.

"Um, Rebecca, you do remember we're doing this as a prank to prove a point, right? Not to actually do it."

"Right. Of course," Rebecca said. She looked a little sheepish, but went back to the book challenging with gusto.

Danny filled out a form for *Frog and Toad Are Friends.* "What's wrong with *Frog and Toad*?" I asked him.

"They're a gay couple," he said.

"Oh, come on," I said. "They are not! They're just friends!"

"That's what *you* say," Danny told me with an evil grin. "To me it's the subversive promotion of a gay life-style."

And that was it, wasn't it? All the book challenges, the real ones, were because one person saw a book in a very different way than somebody else. Which was fine. Everybody had the right to interpret any book any way they wanted to. What they couldn't do then was tell everybody else their interpretation was the *only* interpretation.

Three days later, we had Request for Reconsideration forms filled out for five hundred books. There were lots more books than that in the library, of course, but it was the best we could do, even with Rebecca's lawyer superpowers.

Five hundred book challenges would still look great on TV though, and make our point for us. We were ready.

And then, disaster struck.

And by disaster, I mean my little sisters, which amounts to the same thing.

Embracing the Chaos

That afternoon, I embraced the chaos at home. I danced with my dad as he sang *The Marriage of Figaro*. I played chase with Flotsam and Jetsam. Not even Alexis doing ballet in our room and Angelina running around on all fours like a horse bothered me. Before dinner I sat down at the kitchen table and plowed through my homework without being told to, and I didn't even mind doing fractions for math. Nothing could ruin my good mood. Tomorrow night, Rebecca and Danny and Trey and I were going to show the school board how stupid they were for banning books. We were going to show everybody.

When it was time for dinner, I cleared my books and took them back to my room. As I passed Angelina's room, I had to stop and shake my head in wonder. Angelina had turned her bedroom into another stable, but this one was crazy. There was shredded white recycled paper/pretend hay *everywhere*—on her bookshelves, sticking out of her dresser drawers, in her bed. More than I'd ever seen before.

She was going to *howl* when Mom and Dad made her clean it up, but the tantrum she was going to throw later didn't even make me want to run away. I didn't want to be anywhere else tomorrow night. But it did remind me there was one small detail in our big plan for the school board meeting I hadn't covered yet.

"I need a ride to the school board meeting tomorrow night," I said at dinner.

My parents looked across the table at each other, talking to each other without talking again.

"Are you sure that's such a good idea, Amy Anne?" Mom said.

I slumped in my chair. That's what they always said when they disagreed with me, like I would change my mind if I just thought about it more. But I'd thought about it plenty. And I said so.

"You said you wanted me to stand up for myself more," I told them. "But that I had to do it the right way. Well, the right way is to go to the school board meeting and tell them that banning books is wrong."

Mom and Dad looked at each other again. I could see them waffling.

"You said yourself you didn't agree with the book banning," I said. "If nobody goes there and says anything about it, they'll just keep doing it."

Dad sighed. "Tomorrow night's awfully busy," he said. "Alexis has ballet, Angelina has book club . . ."

"Alexis always has ballet. And Angelina can't even read. They can miss one night."

My sisters erupted.

"I can't miss a single practice!" Alexis protested. "Mrs. Dupond says missing just one class—"

"I can too read! I can read *Chicka Chicka Boom Boom*!" Angelina said, and she launched into reciting it to prove her point.

"Enough—enough!" Dad told them. "You're both excused."

Alexis started to argue again, but Dad assured her we would figure everything out and sent her away. She stomped off to our room to use my bedpost as a ballet barre and Angelina wandered off singing the *Chicka Chicka Boom Boom* song.

Mom leaned down and rubbed her forehead. "I suppose we asked for this," she said.

"There are going to be television cameras there tomorrow night, Amy Anne," Dad said. "Are you sure you want to do this?"

I knew what he meant. I hadn't gone up to the podium the last time he'd taken me, when there was almost nobody there. There were going to be lots more people there tomorrow night, and lots more watching at home on TV. A little monster started gnawing at the insides of my stomach, making me cringe. But I wasn't going to be a good girl and stay quiet. Not this time.

I nodded. I was sure.

"All right," Mom said. "We'll find a way to get you there."

I breathed a big sigh of relief. Everything was set for our big night. I'd promised Trey I'd call him later, but first I wanted to add a few more Request for Reconsideration forms to the big box of them I kept in my room.

But when I got there, the box was gone.

Disaster

I panicked, looking under the bed, on my book-shelves, in my backpack. But the box wasn't in any of those places. I remembered very clearly leaving it on the floor beside my bed, and now it wasn't there.

I marched up to Alexis, who was holding onto my bedpost and doing ballet exercises. "Where are my Request for Reconsideration forms?"

"Your what?" she asked, still mad about me suggesting she could miss a ballet class.

"The big box of papers that was right here beside my bed before I went into the kitchen to do my homework," I told her.

"Oh, that," she said. She swung her leg out in a wide circle. "I moved it so I'd have room to practice my *rond de jambe*."

"*Where* did you move it?"

"Mom's office," she said. "With all the other boxes of paper."

I tromped down the hall to the office/exercise room/ guest bedroom/storage room, mad that Alexis had touched my stuff. The box was there, just like she said it would be.

But it was empty.

"Alexis!" I yelled. "Alexis, what'd you do with the Request for Reconsideration forms!?"

Alexis came out of our room. "I told you! I put them in Mom's office!"

"The box is here, but it's empty!" I told her.

"Well, it wasn't when I put it in there!"

That's when I realized where the empty box was sitting.

Right. Beside. The shredder.

"No," I said. *"No no no no no!"*

Mom came out of the living room. "What's all this yelling?" she asked.

I ran past her into Angelina's room, where she was nestled down in the huge piles of shredded paper like a horse asleep in the hay. I snatched up a handful of the shredded paper and yanked it apart, trying to read what was written on the thin little strips.

"Hey! That's my hay!" Angelina yelled.

I grabbed another handful. And another. They were full of chopped-up black typewriting and handwriting scrawled in blue and black ink. At the top of one were the letters REQ. At the bottom of another was the end of my signature—*ger*. No. No!

"That's mine!" Angelina screamed. "That's mine! You can't touch it! It's mine!"

I threw the shredded paper on the floor and grabbed Angelina by the shirt. "This isn't recycled paper! You shredded up my Request for Reconsideration forms!"

Angelina wailed like I had hit her, which only made me want to more. But before I could do anything else to her Mom and Dad and Alexis were in the doorway.

"What's going on here?" Dad said.

"Everything's ruined. Ruined! She shredded up all our Request for Reconsideration forms! That was the whole point of going to the school board meeting tomorrow! Our whole plan! It took us a week to fill all those out, and now they're ruined!"

I kicked at the piles of shredded paper, sending them flying in the air like snow. Angelina dropped to the floor and sobbed.

"I hate you!" I screamed at her. "I hate you all! I hate this stupid house and everybody in it!"

"Amy Anne!" Mom said.

Alexis and the dogs shrank back from me as I ran past my parents and down the hall to my room. That was it. I was done. I was leaving.

I pulled the little suitcase I used when we went to Granny's house out of my closet and threw it on the bed. I tossed in shirts and skirts and underwear and socks, my favorite stuffed animal, the little statue of Belle I'd bought at Disney World last year, the reading medal I'd won in second grade, what little money I had left over from the B.B.L.L. book-buying account, and a few of my favorite books—including *From the Mixed-up Files of Mrs. Basil E. Frankweiler.* I didn't know where I was going, but I didn't care, so long as it was nowhere near my awful house.

"Amy Anne is packing her suitcase!" Alexis yelled from our doorway. She looked frightened. Behind her, the dogs paced nervously, their tails down. *Good,* I thought. I hoped they all missed me when I was gone.

I zipped up my suitcase and dragged it down the hall. "I'm running away!" I announced.

Alexis started sobbing behind me, but Mom and Dad didn't cry or try to stop me. That just made me madder. I stomped down the hall toward the front door, but Angelina came flying out of her room and wrapped herself around one of my legs.

"No! No, Amy Anne, don't go! I'm sorry I used your papers! I'm sorry! Don't go!" she cried.

I tried to kick Angelina off but she was too big, so I dragged her along like I was wearing a ball and chain. Angelina wailed and clung to me tighter.

Dad crossed his arms and leaned against Angelina's door frame. "Don't you think you're overreacting just a little bit, Amy Anne?"

I stopped. I had so much I wanted to say to that, to say to all of them. The good girl Amy Anne would have said it in her head. But I was done being the good girl, so I said it out loud.

"No," I said. "No, I am *not* overreacting. I'm the one who always has to do things I don't want to do so everybody else will be happy. It's 'Amy Anne, set the table.' 'Amy Anne, let your sister use your books as fences.' 'Amy Anne, let your sister use your bed.' But when *I* want something, it's 'Amy Anne, just be a good girl and let it go.'

"I'm tired of sitting on the sunny side of the car because Alexis is too hot. I'm tired of eating pudding for dessert because Angelina has to have the last cookie. I'm tired of always watching *My Little Pony* instead of *Little House on the Prairie.* I'm tired of doing my homework in the bathroom because Alexis has turned my room into a ballet studio and you're watching TV in the living room and Angelina is using the kitchen table as a pony stable! And I'm tired of people moving my stuff and shredding my papers up to make fake hay and *ruining everything!*"

I peeled the crying Angelina off my leg and pushed her to the wall.

"Why do you think I pretended to be in clubs and stayed late after school every day?" I threw at my parents. *"Because I hate this house and everybody in it!"*

I marched down the hall before Angelina could latch on again, and the dogs slinked out of my way. No one said a word as I slammed the door closed behind me.

Runaway

I had made it as far as the four-lane road outside our subdivision when Mom found me. She pulled up alongside me in the car and rolled down the window.

"Amy Anne, come home," she said.

"No," I said.

"Where are you going to go?"

"To Rebecca's house," I told her, even though I'd just thought of it and didn't know how to get there. All I really wanted to do was get as far away from my house as I could.

A car honked at Mom for sitting in the right lane, and she drove ahead and pulled into the next driveway. She got out and was standing next to the car when I walked up. She and the car were blocking my way.

"Your little sister is a mess," Mom said. "She thinks you're never coming back."

"Good," I told her. "I'm not."

"They didn't mean it, you know," Mom said. "They

didn't know what they were doing, either of them. They didn't ruin your papers on purpose."

"But they did. They ruin everything, and they never get in trouble for it. It's not fair!" I could feel myself starting to cry again, and I hiccupped a sob.

Mom bent down. "Come here," she said. She pulled me into her arms, and I cried into her shoulder. "I wish you hadn't stomped and yelled, but you're right. You do make lots of allowances for your sisters. Your dad and I appreciate it, but sometimes we forget and take it for granted. We're sorry too."

"I'm sorry I said I hate you," I told her. "I don't hate you."

"I know, sweetheart. I know. Will you come home?"

I sobbed again. I didn't want to give up, but I didn't really know where I was going to go or how I was going to live without my family and my home. Running away was so easy for Claudia and Jamie, but they were characters in a book, not real like me. I nodded into her shoulder.

At home, Angelina and Alexis and the dogs practically knocked me down at the door. Angelina and Alexis threw their arms around me and hugged me tight.

"I'm sorry I moved your box without asking," Alexis said.

"I'm sorry I shredded your papers," Angelina said.

It sounded like Dad had coached them on their apologies, but I still appreciated it. Dad hugged me too, and told me he was glad I had decided not to run away after all.

"Can we print new forms for you?" Dad asked. "Your mom can run you by her office tonight, if it will help. Were they something to do with the school board meeting tomorrow night?"

"Yes," I said, still sniffling. "But it's too late."

"We made new papers for you!" Angelina said.

She and Alexis handed me pieces of paper where they had drawn wobbly lines and filled them in with random words. Alexis's were full of ballet terms she had written out by herself. Angelina's were full of the names of *My Little Pony* characters Alexis had written in for her. I knew they were just trying to help, but it made me upset all over again. I was going to have to call Trey and tell him it was over.

"If Mommy makes more we can help you fill them out!" Angelina said.

"No, you don't understand," I said. There wasn't any way to explain to them that lists of ponies and ballet positions weren't going to help. "They have to be filled out at school. And even if Mom was able to copy a thousand of them, we would need every kid at Shelbourne Elementary to fill one out tomorrow by the end of the day."

I suddenly got goosebumps again—but the good kind,

like R. L. Stine goosebumps. That was it. That was the answer!

"Could you?" I asked Mom. "Make lots of copies tonight? Make a thousand copies?"

"Well, yes," Mom said. "We can go right now."

Angelina and Alexis started jumping up and down, sensing my excitement, and the dogs yipped happily.

"Okay. Okay, let me print one up from online and we can go," I said. "No—wait. I need to make a phone call first."

I ran to the kitchen and called Trey to tell him what happened.

"She shredded every single one of them!?" Trey said. He forgot he was supposed to be quiet so his mom didn't hear him. "*She shredded every single one of them?*" he whispered. "But we needed those for *tomorrow's* school board meeting! The four of us can't fill all those out again in time, and by next month it will be too late. There won't be any TV crews there next time. Nobody will care by then."

"I know," I told him. "Which is why we're going to get *everybody in the school* to fill them back out for us."

"How?" Trey asked. "We could only fill those out when we were in the library. Even if we got library passes, we'd have to be in class the rest of the day."

"Which is why we're going to run away from school," I said, butterflies flittering in my stomach. "Like Claudia and Jamie in *From the Mixed-up Files*!"

"Play hooky from school?" Trey asked in an excited whisper. "And go where?"

I laughed. "Where I always run away to," I told him. "The bathroom."

Malaria from Watermelons

Trey and I explained everything to Danny and Rebecca on the bus, and we hid behind them as we came into school the next morning, making sure no teachers saw us before we slipped into the bathrooms—the girls' bathroom for me, the boys' bathroom for Trey. I scurried into the last stall, hung my backpack on the hook, and locked myself in.

My day of playing hooky from school at school had begun.

In *From the Mixed-up Files of Mrs. Basil E. Frankweiler,* Claudia and Jamie leave their band instruments at home and pack all the clothes and money and toothbrushes and things they'll need when they run away in their empty instrument cases. I wasn't in the band, and neither was Trey, so we couldn't do the same thing. But we weren't staying overnight anyway. All I had packed in my backpack was the huge pile of Request for Reconsideration forms my parents had printed off for me the night before, and enough snacks to make it through an entire day.

The first bell rang, and I felt the first pangs of guilt for breaking the rules. When the second bell rang, the one that said I was now officially late to class, I actually shook, afraid that at any moment Detective Banazewski was going to come into the girls' bathroom with a sniffer dog and discover me.

The door to the bathroom opened, and I lifted my legs up and held my breath. What if it was Principal Banazewski, come to look for me? But wait—did that mean I should put my feet down, so I just looked like a regular girl going to the bathroom? Maybe I should rattle the toilet paper around and flush the toilet. No—then she'd expect me to come out of the stall!

"Amy Anne? Are you in here?" somebody whispered. I recognized the voice right away—it was Janna Park! The girl who'd called me AA!

"Here," I whispered, opening the stall door and peeking outside.

Janna had every one of the *Little House on the Prairie* books stacked up in her arms.

"Whoa!" I said. "You even checked out the doubles they had on the shelf."

"Rebecca said to," Janna told me. "She said if we didn't, we might accidentally double up, and we didn't have time for that."

Rebecca. So smart! "Okay," I said, pulling one of the Request for Reconsideration forms from my backpack. "Now I just need you to fill out a form for each book before you go back to class."

Janna began to fill out the first form. "But what do I say? There's nothing bad about *Little House on the Prairie*."

She was right. But no—that was true about all the books. I had to think like Mrs. Spencer. Better, I had to think like *Rebecca*.

"They get malaria in that one," I said. "That's scary, right? And the settlers think it's because they ate bad watermelon! But that's not how you get malaria. That's deliberately misleading. That could make a kid think you get malaria from watermelons!"

Janna giggled and wrote it in.

This was the plan. We were going to do exactly what Mrs. Spencer had done when she wanted to ban books but didn't want to wait for the School Board to say yes. We were going to check out as many books from the library as we could, and then turn in Request for Reconsideration forms for them all tonight at the School Board meeting. Rebecca and Danny stayed on the outside, slipping notes into everybody's lockers that told them to check out books and bring them to me in the girls' bathroom and Trey in the boys' bathroom. That's why we were "playing hooky" from school—so we could be here all day to help them fill out Request for Reconsideration forms for all the books. If even half the kids at Shelbourne Elementary did it, we'd have hundreds of books banned by the end of the day.

The door opened, and a third grader I didn't know came in with a stack of Bunnicula books. "Is this where I go to ban books?" she asked.

"Right this way," I told her. "Let me get you a form."

When You Gotta Go, You Gotta Go

Rebecca came to see me right before lunch, which was good because I needed help. The bathroom was full of girls from third, fourth, fifth, and sixth grade, all carrying stacks of books and filling out forms. They'd all gotten bathroom passes from their different homerooms and come to the bathroom at the same time!

"It's hysterical," Rebecca told me as she helped a third grader fill out her form. "Every time somebody comes back from the bathroom, somebody immediately raises their hand to ask if they can go. And you should see the library. Half the books are gone from the shelves! There's a line of kids checking out armfuls of books. The new lady, the Not–Mrs. Jones, she's about to have a heart attack! She hasn't had any time to read her celebrity magazines, but she can't get mad because checking out books is her job!"

A library without books in it. Just the thought of it gave me the shivers, but that was exactly the point. We were going to show them that once you banned one book, you could ban them all, and then there wouldn't be any books left to read.

"Check them out. Check them *all* out," I told Rebecca. "Oh, and we need more copies of the Request for Reconsideration form."

That meant we had already challenged almost a thousand books! That was way more than Rebecca and Danny and Trey and I had been able to do by ourselves.

"I'll get Danny on it," she said. "He checked in with Trey. He's over there banning as many books as you are! You know Jeffrey Gonzalez? Space Cadet Jeff? I helped him come up with reasons to ban each and every one of the Star Wars books."

"For what?"

"Are you kidding? The Rebel Alliance are basically terrorists. They blow up the *Death Star* at the end of Star Wars. You know how many people must have been on that station? Thousands. That's mass murder!"

The bathroom door clunked open, and the voice I'd dreaded hearing all day boomed loud to be heard over the chatter.

"What's going on in here?" Principal Banazewski said.

I squeaked and dragged Rebecca with me into the last stall on the end. We could hear the sound of footsteps as half the girls in the bathroom hid in the stalls and the other half ran for the exit.

"Every teacher tells me there's a sudden run on the bathroom today," Principal Banazewski said, walking up and down in front of the closed stall doors. She knocked on one of the other stall doors. "What are you doing in there?"

"Um, just going to the bathroom," Sophia Marin said from inside the stall.

The principal's footsteps came closer to our stall. I pushed Rebecca down on the toilet seat and hopped in her lap in case Detective Banazewski started looking under the stall doors. Rebecca winced.

Principal Banazewski knocked on the door of our stall, making us both jump. "Who's in here?"

Rebecca and I looked at each other in horror. Finally I nudged her. She had to be the one to talk. I was supposed to be home sick!

"Um, Rebecca Zimmerman," she said.

"Rebecca, I think it's time you got back to class."

Rebecca and I shared a panicked look.

"But . . . I have a pass," Rebecca said.

"I think you've been gone from class long enough," Principal Banazewski said.

The lunch bell rang, making us jump again, and the hallway outside filled with the sound of squeaking shoes, slamming lockers, and laughing students.

"Well, now that it's lunch period, I'm not *technically* missing class anymore," Rebecca said. She really was going to make a great lawyer one day.

Principal Banazewski sighed as more girls poured into the bathroom. Like Mirror Mrs. Jones in the library, she really couldn't get mad at students using the bathroom during lunch. That's when we were supposed to use the bathroom.

"From now on, please wait until lunchtime to use the bathroom if you can, Miss Zimmerman."

"Yes, ma'am," Rebecca said in her sweetest voice.

We waited until Principal Banazewski was gone, and Rebecca and I slumped back against the toilet in relief.

"Tell everybody to cool it with the bathroom requests," I told her as she slipped out of the stall and the next book banner slipped inside. "And don't forget to get me more forms!"

Good Intentions

When Trey, Rebecca, and Danny and I met up after school, we had so many Request for Reconsideration forms we had to split them up between us to get them home.

"There must be five thousand banned books here, easy!" Trey said.

"Count them up tonight. I want to know," Rebecca said.

"Dude, the library looks like a tornado hit it," Danny said. "There's hardly anything left in the fiction section."

It was crazy. The four of us had only been able to fill out five hundred forms in four days. In one day, with the help of all the other kids at school, we'd blown the roof off that number. We were going to be plunking down a three-foot-tall stack of Request for Reconsideration forms in front of the school board members. Mrs. Spencer wasn't going to know what hit her.

"So we're all going to be there tonight, right?" I asked.

We made sure everyone had a ride and said our good-byes until tonight. Even though I carried ten pounds of paper in my backpack, I felt like I was walking on air as I made my way down to the second grade hall to meet up with Alexis. She usually took the first bus home while I took the late bus, but all that was over now that my parents had figured out I wasn't really staying behind to be part of an after-school club. I was going to have to start taking the early bus with Alexis. But that was next week. This week, Mom and Dad were taking turns picking us up from school.

Alexis was on the little kids' playground, climbing around on the monkey bars. I hadn't been out here since I was little, and everything was different. All the old junky equipment had been replaced by new stuff. It was like a little playground city. New swings, two new slides—one double wide—a curlicue to climb up and a pole to slide down, monkey bars to swing across, and a little gazebo-like thing with a spinning tic-tac-toe game on it. There were even these little speaking tubes sticking up out of the ground. You could talk into one side, and hear it across the playground. And covering the old hard dirt ground that used to turn to mud when it rained was a thick layer of chopped-up rubber pieces. It squished when you walked on it.

The new playground was pretty great. I wished we'd had it when I was in second grade. I read the sign next to the entrance. Donated in memory of Mrs. Emily Briggs by the Shelbourne Elementary PTA, Mrs. Sarah Spencer, President.

Mrs. Sarah Spencer. Trey's mom. The book banner. She'd raised money for a new lower-school playground as president of the Parent-Teacher Association. I stood and stared at the sign for a long time. How was the woman who banned books from the library the same person who bought the little kids a new playground?

Dad pulled up and honked the horn. I waved to him and yelled, "Alexis! Dad's here!"

Alexis ran up, red faced.

"Cool playground," I said.

"It's the best playground ever!" she said.

"Got your book bag?" I reminded her. She found it, and we climbed into Dad's truck. I stared out the window at the shiny new playground equipment as we pulled away.

Donated by the Shelbourne Elementary PTA, Mrs. Sarah Spencer, President. It had been so easy to think of Mrs. Spencer as a villain, but coming up with all those reasons to ban books had made me start to see things from her point of view. It didn't mean I thought she was right. But I was beginning to see how she must have thought she was doing something good for us, even though she was wrong.

In Which I Speak Up

The room where the school board met was a very different place this time.

All the seats on both sides of the aisle were filled, and a partition had to be taken down and new chairs brought in to fit everybody. Most of the kids from my class were there with at least one of their parents, and I saw kids from other classes and other grades there too. Two local camera crews were set up along the back wall, and they were already doing interviews with some of the kids who came. One of them recognized me when I came in with my family, but Dad put up a hand and said, "No comment."

I did have a comment. Lots of comments, in fact. But I was saving them for the meeting.

Mrs. Jones was there, wearing a big pink-and-white polka-dotted dress, and she broke away from an interview she was doing with a reporter to come over and swallow me in a giant hug.

"Oh, Amy Anne! It's so good to see you," she said.

I immediately teared up. "Mrs. Jones—I'm so sorry! I didn't mean to get you fired!"

"It's not your fault at all," Mrs. Jones said. "I couldn't go on the way things were much longer anyhow. I knew it was coming. I'm very proud of what you did, and I don't want you to regret it one bit."

"But I got in trouble. I got a lot of people in trouble," I said.

"Well-behaved women seldom make history," Mrs. Jones said with a smile. "Consider this your first taste of behaving badly in the name of what's right." She hugged me again. "Are you planning on talking tonight?" she asked me.

"I'm already signed up," I told her.

She nodded her approval and then excused herself to go back to her interview.

On the far side of the room, I saw Mrs. Spencer take a seat. She was wearing another pretty skirt and jacket, light blue this time. And right beside her was Trey—wearing a tie! I couldn't believe it. He caught me looking at him, and gave me a little thumbs-up sign where his mom couldn't see it.

Rebecca ran up to me while our parents said hello to each other. She'd dressed up too. She was wearing gray slacks and a gray jacket, with a white button-down shirt underneath.

"You have a suit?" I asked.

"Of course," Rebecca said. "Every lawyer needs a good suit."

I was feeling distinctly underdressed. I was just wearing one of my sundresses, with a ribbon tied around one of my braids.

"You got yours?" Rebecca asked.

I patted the backpack sitting in my chair. "Yep," I said. "You?"

Rebecca hefted a big briefcase and smiled.

The meeting was called to order, and Mom, Dad, Alexis, Angelina, and I found seats. Mom and Dad had decided to bring all of us, and Alexis in particular wasn't happy about it. She was missing ballet practice to be here, and she plopped herself down in her seat with her arms crossed to show us how she felt. She was a grouch, but after my blowup last night she at least wasn't complaining out loud about it.

The school board read out what had happened last time (when I wasn't there) and talked about what they were going to talk about tonight.

Then it was time for public comment.

I took a deep breath. My name was first on the list. I'd made sure of it. I stood, my legs shaking worse than when I'd been called to the principal's office that first time, and my mom squeezed my hand in support. I hadn't been able to do this the first time I'd been to a school board meeting, but I was going to do it now. I nodded to

Rebecca and Danny, and they stood to join me at the podium. Mrs. Spencer was shocked when Trey stood up and joined us too.

"Only one speaker at a time, please," one of the school board members said.

"I'll do all the talking then," I told them. My heart felt like it was in my throat and it was hard to squeeze the words out past it, but it got easier the more I did it. "I'm Amy Anne Ollinger, president and chief librarian of the B.B.L.L."

"The B.B.L.L.?" a school board member asked.

"The Banned Books Locker Library."

That caused a ripple of comment throughout the audience, and I could feel the bright lights of the television cameras on me. It was almost too much. I wanted to duck down underneath the podium and never come out again, but I clung to the sides of it instead, using it to hold me up.

The chairman of the school board banged his gavel for quiet. "We're not going to hear any more arguments for keeping removed books on the shelf," he told us. "We've already had that discussion."

"No . . ." I said. "We're not here to try to get those books back," I said. "We're here with more challenges."

That was the cue. Danny, Trey, and I opened our backpacks, and Rebecca opened her briefcase. Each of us pulled out a huge pile of papers and carried them up to the round table at the front, stacking them on top of each other so they would look really impressive. Behind us, I could hear cameras snapping, and more whispers and questions.

"What is this?" the chairman asked.

I went back to the microphone. "Request for Reconsideration forms," I told him. "We think there are more books we shouldn't be able to read."

The school board members started taking sheets from the big stack. Each one was for a different book. I'd made sure.

"But—there must be thousands of books here!" one of them said.

"Seven thousand, five hundred, and forty-one," I said. It wasn't every book in the library—not even half—but it had put a serious dent in the shelves.

That number got a big response from the audience, and the chairman had to gavel them quiet again.

"These are a joke," one of the school board members said. "You want to ban a math textbook?"

"It has imaginary numbers in it," I said. "We're afraid that will encourage kids to have imaginary friends."

The audience laughed, and I felt better about talking. My hands relaxed on the podium.

"Here's one challenging the dictionary," said another board member.

Danny leaned in to the microphone. "Oh, that book

is full of dirty words. I looked all of them up." He turned to the cameras behind him, ran his fingers through his hair, and smiled a million dollar smile. "Danny Purcell," he said. "Two *N*s, two *L*s."

"*Magic Tree House*?" said another board member. "Challenged for . . . building code violations?"

Mrs. Spencer stood in a huff. "Your Honors, this is clearly a joke. Can we move on?"

My dad stood up. "Oh, no," he said. "I work in construction, and I've seen those books. That tree house doesn't have any handrails, and you can see from the picture those floor joists aren't anywhere near twelve inches apart."

That got another laugh and stirred everybody up again.

"Mr. Chairman!" Mrs. Spencer called over the ruckus. "Mr. Chairman, I move that these new challenges be ignored so we can get on to real business."

"You can't make a motion during public comment," Rebecca said into the microphone. "Besides, she's not even supposed to be talking. You said only one speaker at a time."

"And who are you?" the chairman asked.

"Rebecca Zimmerman. Legal counsel for the B.B.L.L.," Rebecca said importantly.

"Then surely her time is up," Mrs. Spencer said.

The chairman looked relieved. "It is up. I'm afraid you're going to have to take a seat, Miss Ollinger. It's . . ."

He consulted his list, and his voice turned weary. "Rebecca Zimmerman's turn to speak."

Rebecca leaned in to the microphone. "I respectfully cede my remaining time to Amy Anne Ollinger."

The chairman of the school board covered his mike, but everyone in the room could hear him ask the other members, "Can she do that? Is that allowed?"

"It's in *Robert's Rules of Order*," Rebecca told him. "And the next twelve names are all Shelbourne Elementary students who are going to cede their time to Amy Anne, so you're going to have to listen to what she has to say."

The kids who'd signed up to speak stood up, scattered in different rows around the room. Rebecca's mom and dad, both wearing suits, gave her big smiles and double thumbs-up.

"Your Honor," I said, charging ahead before they could tell me to sit down, "you have to ban these books."

"We have to do no such thing," the chairman said. "Most of these challenges are for silly reasons."

"Silly to you, maybe. All reasons are silly to someone else, and we think the challenges to the books already removed are silly. What makes one person's reason any sillier than another person's reason?"

That got them quiet, and the quiet made me nervous again. I desperately wanted to suck on my braids, but I knew I couldn't. Not here. I gripped the podium harder. "You took *The Egypt Game* off the library shelves because one person didn't like the kids pretending to worship an Egyptian god. You took the Junie B. Jones books off the shelf because one person didn't like the way she talks. You took my favorite book in the whole wide world, *From the Mixed-up Files of Mrs. Basil E. Frankweiler,* off the shelf because *one person* said it taught kids how to lie and cheat and run away from home, even though I never cheated on anything."

I hoped they wouldn't notice I'd left out *lie and run away from home,* and pushed on.

"You can't have it both ways. If you banned those books because just one person had a problem with them, you have to ban all these books too, because we found one person who had a problem with each of them. And when you're done, there isn't going to be a single book left on the Shelbourne Elementary shelves. But I guess that's okay with you. The Wake County School Board doesn't want its students to read any books that scare them, or teach them, or entertain them, or show them new things, or make them sad, or happy, or shock them, or open their minds. Which is all of them."

The room was dead quiet now, except for the hum of the TV cameras. The school board members looked pale under the fluorescent lights in the ceiling. Or maybe that was because of the TV cameras too.

Mrs. Spencer spoke up. She had never sat down. "This is silly," she said. "Those books were removed from the

Shelbourne Elementary library for good reason—because they were harmful. Each and every one of them encouraged bad behavior of one kind or another, and I think we can all agree that none of us want an entire generation of Shelbourne Elementary students growing up to be menaces to society, just because some book they read in fourth grade showed them how."

Rebecca was about to say something, probably to remind the school board that there was only supposed to be one speaker at a time, but I put a hand on her arm to stop her.

"So all those books you challenged," I said to Mrs. Spencer, "if I read one of those, I would grow up to be a bad person?"

"I'd say the chances are good, yes."

I was ready for this. I could feel every eye in the room on me, waiting to hear what I would say. Waiting for me, Amy Anne Ollinger, to speak up.

"Mrs. Spencer, one of the first books you banned was *Are You There God? It's Me, Margaret.* Have you ever read it?"

One or two people in the room coughed. They knew the book talked about embarrassing stuff, stuff you didn't talk about in a big room full of people. Stuff like the things that happen to a girl's body when she becomes a teenager.

Mrs. Spencer blushed. "No. Of course not."

I looked right at her. "Are you sure?"

Mrs. Spencer raised herself up. "I'm sure I didn't."

"That's funny," I said. "Because I've got this old date due card from the Shelbourne Elementary copy, and it's got your signature on here from 1982."

The audience gasped and giggled as I held up the card I'd found in the back of the library's old copy of *Are You There God? It's Me, Margaret.* The color drained from Mrs. Spencer's face.

"Well, I—I might have checked it out once, but when I saw what it was, I didn't read it," Mrs. Spencer said.

"Five times?" I asked. That got a big laugh from the audience. The TV reporters were loving it! Mrs. Spencer looked sick, and she started to sit down. I didn't like what she'd done, and I wanted to fix it, but I didn't want to punish her.

"Mrs. Spencer, wait," I said. "Mrs. Spencer, is it true you're on the North Carolina Art Museum board?"

Mrs. Spencer looked confused. "I—yes. I am."

"And the Raleigh Race for the Cure Foundation board?"

"Yes."

"And the North Carolina State Opera Society board?"

"Yes," she said, and my dad whistled a little cheer.

"And you were the one who raised money for the new lower-school playground at Shelbourne Elementary," I said.

"Well, yes. There were a lot of people involved with that, but I oversaw it, yes."

"Mrs. Spencer, would you say you're a good person?" I asked.

Mrs. Spencer swallowed like she was trying not to cry. "Yes," she said. "I like to think so."

"I think so too," I told her. "I think you grew up to be a very nice person, and a good mom, and a very good citizen. Even though you read this book you said was so bad five times when you were in fifth grade. Probably because for all the amazing things books can do, they can't make you into a bad person."

Mrs. Spencer sat down to wipe her eyes with a tissue.

The room was quiet again, and everyone was still watching me. The chairman of the school board finally cleared his throat and spoke.

"Miss Ollinger? Do you have anything else?"

"Well, we do have a presentation about the First Amendment, drawn by our challenge response coordinator, Trey McBride," I said.

The chairman held up a hand. "I don't think we need that."

One of the other school board members leaned toward her mike. "I think perhaps we do, Stan." She motioned for Trey to bring them the pictures, and he handed out the presentation he and I had created for Mr. Vaughn's class. The school board passed them around respectfully.

"What's this one with the pope lifting weights?" one of them asked.

"The free exercise of religion," Trey told them.

I gave him an exasperated look.

"What?" he said. "It still works! They can do whatever they want in church, even if it's jerks and squats."

"Thank you, Mr. McBride," said the lady who'd asked for the pictures. He collected them all and came back to the podium, and we waited.

The school board members knew they were in trouble. They either had to ban all the books we were challenging, or they had to ban none of them. Either way, they were going to look like idiots in front of the TV cameras.

Mrs. Jones came to their rescue. She got up and joined us at the podium.

"I think I may have a solution," she said. "If Miss Ollinger will cede some of her time to me?"

I nodded.

"Ladies and gentlemen of the school board, not so long ago, when I was the librarian at Shelbourne Elementary, we had an official policy for book challenges. When a book was challenged, it went to a faculty committee for review, and then to me, your hired representative, for a final decision. It was a fair and balanced system you yourselves designed and approved, and it was a system that protected *everyone* in the process. But none of the books that have been removed from the Shelbourne Elementary shelves ever went through that process. Not one."

One or two of the school board members started to understand where she was going, even if I didn't.

"All this trouble began when the official Request for Reconsideration policy was abandoned, and this board began arbitrarily removing books from the shelves. I humbly submit that we go back to the policy as set down in the school board's bylaws. In doing so, the books originally removed from the Shelbourne Elementary shelves will be returned—pending a full review by the faculty committee and a final decision by the school librarian. Then, if it's determined that the books are inappropriate for students that age, they can be removed. And if not . . ."

Mrs. Jones trailed off, but we all knew what would happen. What was going to happen. The books would stay on the Shelbourne Elementary shelves, and everyone who had banned them to begin with would get a great big do-over. And this time, they wouldn't make the same mistake twice.

"Move to submit all challenged books through the Reconsideration Policy as set forth in the school board bylaws," one of the board members said.

"Second!" three more of them said quickly.

"All those in favor?" asked the chairman.

"Aye," they all said quickly. He didn't even ask if there

were any opposed. He banged his gavel, and the room erupted in cheers.

I grabbed up Danny and Trey and Rebecca in one big hug.

"I don't understand," Danny said. "What's it mean?"

"It means they made a motion during public comment time, which legally you're not supposed to do," Rebecca said.

"Oh hush," I told her. I hopped up and down. "It means we won!"

Agent Double-A

The day after the school board meeting, every local news station and newspaper wanted an interview with me. We even got a call from a national cable news channel. Mom and Dad finally gave in and let me do interviews, but I said the same thing to all of them. It was something Mrs. Jones had said the first day Mrs. Spencer came in to challenge Captain Underpants, and I practiced it over and over until I got it right every time:

"Nobody has the right to tell you what books you can and can't read except your parents."

Mrs. Jones got her job back, and all the books that had been banned from the Shelbourne Elementary library were returned to the shelves for good. Somebody from the local newspaper came out to take a picture of me, Rebecca, Danny, and Trey helping Mrs. Jones put them back.

Before we got started, Mrs. Jones pinned a plastic badge to my shirt. I flipped it up to look at it. It was one of the badges the teachers wore. It had my picture on it, and beside that it said, Amy Anne Ollinger, Assistant Librarian.

"There you go," Mrs. Jones said. "Now it's official. Although, if you're going to be a real librarian, we're going to have to have a talk about library patron privacy. But that's a discussion for another time. Congratulations, Amy Anne. And thank you."

Mrs. Jones swallowed me in a big polka-dotted hug, and Rebecca, Danny, and Trey clapped like I'd won some big award.

Mrs. Jones wheeled out the cart of banned books, and we started putting them back where they belonged while the reporter took pictures. When we got to the end, there were a bunch of stapled books with construction-paper covers that I had never seen before. The title on the first one was *Agent Double-A Versus the Book-Eating Bovine*. There was a picture on the cover of a spy girl with a mask over her eyes, fighting a ninja cow with a book in its mouth. In the top corner, it said "First Amendment Comics."

"Those are some new acquisitions I was hoping you could help me shelve," Mrs. Jones said. "They go in the graphic novels section under *M*, for McBride."

Danny flicked his hair out of his eyes so he could see. "Trey drew this?" he said. "Sweet."

"Agent Double-A, hunh?" Rebecca said. "She looks a lot like you, Amy Anne."

Trey blushed. "I just got inspired."

I grinned. I liked it. Especially because I wasn't a mouse anymore. I was a kick-butt secret agent.

"I'm not sure your mom is going to like being drawn as a cow though," I said.

Trey's eyes went wide. "Oh. Yeah. Well, let's just not tell her."

The End

I admired my new librarian badge as I sat on the first bus home that afternoon with my sister Alexis. The bus let us off at the bottom of our street, and Alexis pirouetted for home. I stood and stared again at my yellow house. I still liked the idea of running away, *From the Mixed-up Files* style, but only for the adventure. I wasn't so reluctant to go home anymore. My house was still Chaos Central. No doubt about that. It was me who was different. I wasn't going to take things lying down anymore. If something bothered me, I was going to say something about it.

"Come on, Amy Anne!" Alexis called, and I hurried to catch up.

Flotsam and Jetsam greeted us at the door, jumping all over us and almost knocking me down. They scrambled away just as quickly, chasing Angelina as she galloped by into the living room. No one was in the kitchen, but

I could hear Dad singing his favorite opera song somewhere down the hall.

"Amy Anne? Are you and Alexis home?" my mom called. That surprised me. Mom wasn't usually home this early.

"Yeah!" I yelled back.

"Come and help us," Mom said. "We're in the guest bedroom."

Great. If they were in the guest bedroom, that probably meant they were cleaning it for somebody to stay in it, and they wanted me to help. Sure enough, when I got there I found Dad pulling boxes out of the closet and Mom taking stuff off her desk.

"Why don't Angelina and Alexis have to help?" I wanted to ask. So I did.

"Because this isn't going to be their bedroom," Mom said. "It's going to be yours."

I was stunned. *My bedroom?* As in, all mine and nobody else's?

Dad lifted a dumbbell. "Your mom and I realized we had a workout room nobody ever worked out in."

"And a home office I never do office work in," Mom said. "And if your grandmother and grandfather come and visit, we can put them in our room and we can sleep on the pull-out couch in the living room. It's high time you and Alexis had your own rooms."

"And maybe now you won't feel like you have to stay

late in the library after school just to avoid coming home," Dad said.

I blushed. "I'm sorry," I told them again.

Mom hugged me. "It's all right, sweetheart. It's not a big house, I know, and it can feel overwhelming sometimes."

"A lot of times," I thought. And I said so.

Mom laughed. "A lot of times. But now you'll have your very own Fortress of Solitude. Here—I've already cleared off a bookcase for you. You can use one shelf for the books you own, and another for the books you check out from the library."

I ran to get my stack of books from my room—my old room—and put them on the shelf one by one. I was going to have to start alphabetizing them by author. Maybe even separate them out by subject. But for now I just stuffed them onto the bookshelf. My very own bookshelf. I filled the shelf beneath the books I owned with the six books I'd brought home that day from the library.

"You checked all of these out today?" Dad asked. He picked up *The Hunger Games* and flipped through it. "Whoa," he said. "This seems pretty violent." He closed it and read the back cover. "It says here the main character is sixteen."

"It was in the elementary school library," I told him.

"Yes, but Shelbourne Elementary goes up to sixth grade," he said. "I think maybe I don't want you reading this one just yet."

I gawked at my dad. "You're—you're *banning that book*? But we just got the school board to *stop* banning books!"

"No," Dad said. "You got the school board to stop banning *everybody* from reading books. As I seem to recall, we're still your parents, and can tell you what you can and can't do."

"But—but Rebecca's parents let *her* read it!" I said.

"Rebecca's parents can let her do whatever they want," Dad said. "How did that cute little girl on the TV put it, hon?" he asked my mom.

"'Nobody has the right to tell you what books you can and can't read. Except your parents,'" Mom said, quoting what I'd said on TV back to me. There wasn't much I could say to that. I was the one who'd said it. And I had to admit: this was *exactly* what I had fought for.

Dad kissed me on the top of my head and put *The Hunger Games* on top of the bookshelf. "Just wait a couple of years. You'll like it better then anyway."

I nodded. I wasn't happy about it, but I respected their decision. Every now and then you had to break the rules to do the right thing, but a lot of times following the rules *was* the right thing.

That made me think of something, and I smiled. Mrs. Spencer had banned my favorite book because she thought it would encourage kids to lie, steal, and be disrespectful to adults, and I had done all of those things. But it wasn't any book that made me do all that; it was *banning* a book that made me lie, steal, and be disrespectful to adults. I thought that was pretty funny, and thought about saying so to my parents.

So I did.

Author's Note

Every book banned by the school board in this novel is the title of a book that has been challenged or banned in an American library at least once in the last thirty years.

Acknowledgments

Thanks for this one go to my agent, Holly Root, for championing *Ban This Book* (the first of what I'm sure will be many, many books together!), and to Susan Chang and Kathleen Doherty at Tor/Starscape for taking a chance on a very different kind of book for me and for them. Thanks to fellow Bat Cavers Gwenda Bond, Elle Cosimano, Megan Miranda, Beth Revis, Carrie Ryan, and Megan Shepherd for reading early chapters, and especially to Rebecca Petruck and Tiffany Trent, who read the whole thing. You all gave me terrific feedback. Thanks to my great friend Bob, and as always to my wife, Wendi, and daughter, Jo. And very special thanks to all the librarians out there who continue to stand up for education, entertainment, and freedom. Keep fighting the good fight!

STARSCAPE BOOKS
Reading & Activity Guide to

Ban This Book

By Alan Gratz

Ages 8–12; Grades 3–7

About this guide

The following questions and activities are intended to enhance your reading of *Ban This Book*. The guide has been developed in alignment with the Common Core State Standards; however, please feel free to adapt this content to suit the needs and interests of your readers.

PREREADING DISCUSSION TOPICS AND ACTIVITIES

1. What does it mean to "ban" something? Have you ever encountered a ban in your home, school, or community? Can you think of something you would like to see banned? Can you think of something that you feel would be terrible to ban? Explain your answers.

2. Family relationships play an important role in this story. Who are the members of your family? Are

you the oldest, youngest, middle, or only child? Do you share a bedroom or study space? Do you have responsibilities, such as watching a baby cousin, or rules, such as staying out of an older sister's bedroom? What are your parents' or guardians' expectations of you? What chore or family activity do you find difficult? What is your favorite thing to do with your family? Write a paragraph describing the best or most unique thing about your family. Illustrate your paragraph with a family photo or drawing.

3. The main character in *Ban This Book* has a favorite book, which she has read many times. Do you have a favorite book? What makes this book special to you? How did you first discover this book? How many times have you read the story? Write a paragraph recommending this book to a friend, classmate, or family member. Explain what the story is about and why you think someone else should read it.

4. How often do you visit your school library? Your local library? What is the last book you checked out of the library? With friends or classmates, make a brainstorm list of important needs you feel libraries serve in your school and community. If possible, visit your local library or go online to learn about upcoming library events you may want to attend with friends or family members.

POSTREADING DISCUSSION QUESTIONS

1. To what does Amy Anne compare her favorite book on the first page of the novel? How does this comparison help you understand the character of Amy herself? What is Amy Anne's favorite book and why does she love it? What do you think your favorite book (or your feelings about reading) might tell people about you?

2. What things trouble Amy Anne about her family life? What advice might you give to Amy Anne about dealing with her sisters and about getting her parents to understand her concerns?

3. What are the main reasons Amy Anne is upset by Mrs. Spencer's decision to remove books from the school library? If you had been a student at Shelbourne Elementary, would you have been upset about this situation? Why or why not?

4. The first School Board meeting happens in the chapter titled "Common Sense." How does the description of the meeting room make you feel? How do Mrs. Jones and Mrs. Spencer challenge each other during the meeting, and what arguments do they use for and against the removal of library books? What does Amy Anne do (or fail to do) before the vote about removing books from the library?

5. With whom is Amy Anne partnered for the Bill of Rights school project? What upsets her about this situation? With whom would she have preferred to be partnered?

6. What is Amy Anne's big idea in the chapter titled "The Big Idea"? Do you think it is a good idea? Why or why not? Which of Amy Anne's classmates help the idea to grow even bigger until it becomes the B.B.L.L.?

7. Were you surprised by Amy Anne's attitude in the chapter titled "The Banana Room"? What thoughts or emotions is Amy experiencing in this scene? What order does Amy Anne receive from Principal Banazewski at the chapter's end? How might you explain the difference between the words "banned" and "removed"?

8. In "Tools of the Trade," what does Amy Anne learn about library science that helps her improve the B.B.L.L.? Later, how does Amy Anne use the library's "Request for Reconsideration" paperwork to make a point about the hazards of banning books? Do any of these elements of the story make you want to consider getting a doctorate in Library Science, like Opal Jones? Explain your answer.

9. Who does Amy Anne hold responsible for getting her suspended? Who is really responsible and why? What emotions does Amy Anne feel when she learns

this truth? What does it teach her about the power of books?

10. What plan does Amy Anne make in the chapter "The Biggest Idea"? Which character surprises her by helping her make this plan?

11. What book does Amy Anne mention to Mrs. Spencer that changes the direction of the second School Board meeting? How did Amy Anne discover Mrs. Spencer's relationship to this book? How does this revelation affect your attitude toward Mrs. Spencer?

12. In what ways can a family be seen as a small community? How are the roles of parents similar to (and different from) the roles of educators in the school community and board members in a town community? What similarities and differences do you see between Amy Anne's family and school communities and your own?

13. Do you agree with Amy Anne's statement that ". . . for all the amazing things books can do, they can't make you into a bad person"? If you agree, then why does anyone believe that books can be dangerous?

14. One important thing the author does is to create a banned books list that includes titles that Amy Anne doesn't like, and even some that she feels uncomfortable reading. Why might this be important to the story? What do you think the author is trying to say about the things people choose to ban?

15. In the course of the novel, Amy Anne learns to speak up for herself. What other characters find ways to better express themselves as the story comes to an end? How does the fight against banning books particularly help these characters find their own strengths? How might *Ban This Book* be read as a story about learning to express oneself through words, art, action, and even in the books we choose to take from a library shelf?

POSTREADING WRITING, RESEARCH, AND COMMUNITY ACTIVITIES

1. POINT-OF-VIEW: *Ban This Book* is told in first-person ("I") by Amy Anne, a character who often finds herself unable to speak up for herself. Make a list of at least four moments in the story where Amy Anne stays silent. For each moment, write a short paragraph describing how the story might have been different had Amy Anne voiced a question or concern, what you think she would have said, and how the story might have changed had she spoken up.

2. THEME: Throughout the novel, the author explores the question of "intentions." What are "good intentions"? Do "good intentions" always lead to good outcomes? What should you do if a person with "good intentions" causes a bad situation? Cite exam-

ples from the story in which Amy Anne, her sisters, friends, and parents unintentionally cause harm. Write a paragraph explaining how Mrs. Spencer, the book-banning mom who school librarian Mrs. Jones also calls "a pillar of our fair community," represents the tension between intentions and outcomes.

3. RESEARCH & PRESENT: DAV PILKEY. In *Ban This Book*, real-life author Dav Pilkey visits Shelbourne Elementary. Go to the library to learn more about Dav and his books, making sure to read his 2014 on-line article entitled, "My Book Makes Kids Laugh, And It Was Banned Anyway" (www.huffingtonpost.com/dav-pilkey/captain-underpants banned-book _b_5863980.html). Create an informational poster about Dav's life and stories. Be sure to include a quote from his article, as well as an illustration of your own.

4. TEXT TYPE: NARRATIVE. In the character of TREY McBRIDE, write a journal entry describing how you feel about Amy Anne's battle with your mom and/or a journal entry about your dream of becoming a comic book artist.

5. RESEARCH & CREATE: BOOK COVERS. In the chapter "What's in a Name," Amy Anne and her friends make up fake book titles, with M.J. designing corresponding covers. Using a graphic design program, colored pencils, or other visual art materials,

create a new cover for your favorite book. Design a cover for one of the books on the American Library Association's List of Challenged Children's Books (www.ala.org/bbooks/frequentlychallenged /childrensbooks). Or, design a cover for Amy Anne's made-up title, *Friend or Foe*. Create a classroom display of your custom-designed covers.

6. TEXT TYPE: OPINION PIECE. The very first amendment to the United States Constitution, which protects citizens' rights to "Freedoms, Petitions, Assembly," reads: "Congress shall make no law respecting an establishment of religion, or prohibiting the free exercise thereof; or abridging the freedom of speech, or of the press, or the right of the people peaceably to assemble, and to petition the Government for a redress of grievances." (www.ushistory .org/documents/amendments.htm). Write a short essay answering the following questions: How do you think this amendment protects libraries specifically, and why it was important to include a mention of this amendment in *Ban This Book*? Does any argument justify limiting these rights? If so, who should have the right to set the limits? How are similar questions resolved in the novel?

7. A READING COMMUNITY. As she works to get banned books back on her school library's shelves, Amy Anne discovers that she is not alone. In fact, she

is part of a community of booklovers that includes friends, classmates, and her school librarian. Can you recognize the booklovers in your home, community, or classroom? Join together to celebrate the printed word. Choose a date and time, and send out invitations. Plan activities, such as a book exchange, dramatic reading, or story character costume contest. Serve hot fudge sundaes (a treat mentioned in Amy Anne's favorite novel, *From the Mixed-Up Files of Mrs. Basil E. Frankweiler*) or other book-themed treats. If desired, spread more book love. Host a book drive for a local family shelter; read aloud to younger siblings or classmates; celebrate Children's Book Week (visit bookweekonline.com/for-kids for details); or make a giant "READ" poster to display in your community.

Supports English Language Arts Common Core State Standards:

RL.3.1-6; RL.4.1-6; RL.5.1-6; RL.5.9; RL.6.1-6; RL.7.1-4, 7.6

SL: 3.1-3; SL.4.1-4; SL.5.1-4; SL.6.1-4; SL.7.1-4

W.3.1-2; W.4.1-2; W.5.1-2; W.6. 1-2; W.7.1-2

About the Author

ALAN GRATZ is the author of many critically acclaimed books for children and teens, including *Samurai Shortstop*, an ALA Top Ten Best Book for Young Adults; *Prisoner B-3087*; *The Brooklyn Nine*; and the League of Seven trilogy (*The League of Seven*, *The Dragon Lantern*, *The Monster War*). A native of Knoxville, Tennessee, Alan is now a full-time writer living in western North Carolina with his wife and daughter. Look for him online at www .alangratz.com, and on Twitter as @AlanGratz.